Henry James OM (15 April 1843 – 28 February 1916) was an American-British author regarded as a key transitional figure between literary realism and literary modernism, and is considered by many to be among the greatest novelists in the English language. He was the son of Henry James Sr. and the brother of renowned philosopher and psychologist William James and diarist Alice James.

He is best known for a number of novels dealing with the social and marital interplay between émigré Americans, English people, and continental Europeans. Examples of such novels include The Portrait of a Lady, The Ambassadors, and The Wings of the Dove. His later works were increasingly experimental. In describing the internal states of mind and social dynamics of his characters, James often made use of a style in which ambiguous or contradictory motives and impressions were overlaid or juxtaposed in the discussion of a character's psyche.(Source: Wikipedia)

Literary works:
Watch and Ward (1871)
Roderick Hudson (1875)
The American (1877)
The Europeans (1878)
Confidence (1879)
Washington Square (1880)
The Portrait of a Lady (1881)
The Bostonians (1886)
The Princess Casamassima (1886)
The Reverberator (1888)
The Tragic Muse (1890)
The Other House (1896)
The Spoils of Poynton (1897)
What Maisie Knew (1897)

PRINCE CLASSICS

THE COXON FUND

HENRY JAMES

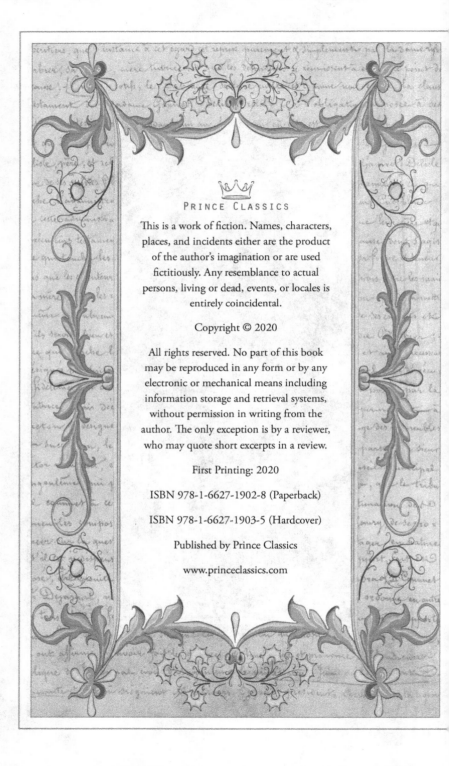

PRINCE CLASSICS

First Printing: 2020

ISBN 978-1-6627-1902-8 (Paperback)

ISBN 978-1-6627-1903-5 (Hardcover)

Published by Prince Classics

www.princeclassics.com

Contents

THE COXON
FUND

I

"THEY'VE got him for life!" I said to myself that evening on my way back to the station; but later on, alone in the compartment (from Wimbledon to Waterloo, before the glory of the District Railway) I amended this declaration in the light of the sense that my friends would probably after all not enjoy a monopoly of Mr. Saltram. I won't pretend to have taken his vast measure on that first occasion, but I think I had achieved a glimpse of what the privilege of his acquaintance might mean for many persons in the way of charges accepted. He had been a great experience, and it was this perhaps that had put me into the frame of foreseeing how we should all, sooner or later, have the honour of dealing with him as a whole. Whatever impression I then received of the amount of this total, I had a full enough vision of the patience of the Mulvilles. He was to stay all the winter: Adelaide dropped it in a tone that drew the sting from the inevitable emphasis. These excellent people might indeed have been content to give the circle of hospitality a diameter of six months; but if they didn't say he was to stay all summer as well it was only because this was more than they ventured to hope. I remember that at dinner that evening he wore slippers, new and predominantly purple, of some queer carpet-stuff; but the Mulvilles were still in the stage of supposing that he might be snatched from them by higher bidders. At a later time they grew, poor dears, to fear no snatching; but theirs was a fidelity which needed no help from competition to make them proud. Wonderful indeed as, when all was said, you inevitably pronounced Frank Saltram, it was not to be overlooked that the Kent Mulvilles were in their way still more extraordinary: as striking an instance as could easily be encountered of the familiar truth that remarkable men find remarkable conveniences.

They had sent for me from Wimbledon to come out and dine, and there had been an implication in Adelaide's note—judged by her notes alone she might have been thought silly—that it was a case in which something momentous was to be determined or done. I had never known them not be in a "state" about somebody, and I dare say I tried to be droll on this point in accepting their invitation. On finding myself in the presence of their lates discovery I had not at first felt irreverence droop—and, thank heaven, I hav never been absolutely deprived of that alternative in Mr. Saltram's company I saw, however—I hasten to declare it—that compared to this specimen thei other phoenixes had been birds of inconsiderable feather, and I afterward took credit to myself for not having even in primal bewilderments mad a mistake about the essence of the man. He had an incomparable gift; never was blind to it—it dazzles me still. It dazzles me perhaps even more ii remembrance than in fact, for I'm not unaware that for so rare a subject th imagination goes to some expense, inserting a jewel here and there or givin a twist to a plume. How the art of portraiture would rejoice in this figui if the art of portraiture had only the canvas! Nature, in truth, had largel rounded it, and if memory, hovering about it, sometimes holds her breath this is because the voice that comes back was really golden.

Though the great man was an inmate and didn't dress, he kept dinner or this occasion waiting, and the first words he uttered on coming into the roon were an elated announcement to Mulville that he had found out something Not catching the allusion and gaping doubtless a little at his face, I privatel asked Adelaide what he had found out. I shall never forget the look she gav me as she replied: "Everything!" She really believed it. At that moment, a any rate, he had found out that the mercy of the Mulvilles was infinite. H had previously of course discovered, as I had myself for that matter, tha their dinners were soignés. Let me not indeed, in saying this, neglect t declare that I shall falsify my counterfeit if I seem to hint that there was ii his nature any ounce of calculation. He took whatever came, but he neve plotted for it, and no man who was so much of an absorbent can ever hav been so little of a parasite. He had a system of the universe, but he had n system of sponging—that was quite hand-to-mouth. He had fine gross eas senses, but it was not his good-natured appetite that wrought confusion. I he had loved us for our dinners we could have paid with our dinners, anc it would have been a great economy of finer matter. I make free in thes connexions with the plural possessive because if I was never able to do wha the Mulvilles did, and people with still bigger houses and simpler charities I met, first and last, every demand of reflexion, of emotion—particularl perhaps those of gratitude and of resentment. No one, I think, paid the tribute of giving him up so often, and if it's rendering honour to borrow wisdom I've a right to talk of my sacrifices. He yielded lessons as the sea yields fish—I lived for a while on this diet. Sometimes it almost appeared to me that his massive monstrous failure—if failure after all it was—had been designed for my private recreation. He fairly pampered my curiosity; but the history of that experience would take me too far. This is not the large canvas I just now spoke of, and I wouldn't have approached him with my present hand had it been a question of all the features. Frank Saltram's features, for artistic purposes, are verily the anecdotes that are to be gathered. Their name is legion, and this is only one, of which the interest is that it concerns even more closely several other persons. Such episodes, as one looks back, are the little dramas that made up the innumerable facets of the big drama—which is yet to be reported.

II

IT is furthermore remarkable that though the two stories are distinct—my own, as it were, and this other—they equally began, in a manner, the first night of my acquaintance with Frank Saltram, the night I came back from Wimbledon so agitated with a new sense of life that, in London, for the very thrill of it, I could only walk home. Walking and swinging my stick, I overtook, at Buckingham Gate, George Gravener, and George Gravener's story may be said to have begun with my making him, as our paths lay together, come home with me for a talk. I duly remember, let me parenthesise, that it was still more that of another person, and also that several years were to elapse before it was to extend to a second chapter. I had much to say to him, none the less, about my visit to the Mulvilles, whom he more indifferently knew, and I was at any rate so amusing that for long afterwards he never encountered me without asking for news of the old man of the sea. I hadn't said Mr. Saltram was old, and it was to be seen that he was of an age to outweather George Gravener. I had at that time a lodging in Ebury Street, and Gravener was staying at his brother's empty house in Eaton Square. At Cambridge, five years before, even in our devastating set, his intellectual power had seemed to me almost awful. Some one had once asked me privately, with blanched cheeks, what it was then that after all such a mind as that left standing. "It leaves itself!" I could recollect devoutly replying. I could smile at present for this remembrance, since before we got to Ebury Street I was struck with the fact that, save in the sense of being well set up on his legs, George Gravener had actually ceased to tower. The universe he laid low had somehow bloomed again—the usual eminences were visible. I wondered whether he had lost his humour, or only, dreadful thought, had never had any—not even when I had fancied him most Aristophanesque. What was the need of appealing to laughter, however, I could enviously enquire, where you might appeal so confidently to measurement? Mr. Saltram's queer figure, his thick nose and hanging lip, were fresh to me: in the light of my old friend's fine cold symmetry they presented mere success in amusing as the refuge of conscious ugliness.

Already, at hungry twenty-six, Gravener looked as blank and parliamentary as if he were fifty and popular. In my scrap of a residence—he had a worldling's eye for its futile conveniences, but never a comrade's joke—I sounded Frank Saltram in his ears; a circumstance I mention in order to note that even then I was surprised at his impatience of my enlivenment. As he had never before heard of the personage it took indeed the form of impatience of the preposterous Mulvilles, his relation to whom, like mine, had had its origin in an early, a childish intimacy with the young Adelaide, the fruit of multiplied ties in the previous generation. When she married Kent Mulville, who was older than Gravener and I and much more amiable, I gained a friend, but Gravener practically lost one. We reacted in different ways from the form taken by what he called their deplorable social action—the form (the term was also his) of nasty second-rate gush. I may have held in my 'for intérieur' that the good people at Wimbledon were beautiful fools, but when he sniffed at them I couldn't help taking the opposite line, for I already felt that even should we happen to agree it would always be for reasons that differed. It came home to me that he was admirably British as, without so much as a sociable sneer at my bookbinder, he turned away from the serried rows of my little French library.

"Of course I've never seen the fellow, but it's clear enough he's a humbug."

"Clear 'enough' is just what it isn't," I replied; "if it only were!" That ejaculation on my part must have been the beginning of what was to be later a long ache for final frivolous rest. Gravener was profound enough to remark after a moment that in the first place he couldn't be anything but a Dissenter, and when I answered that the very note of his fascination was his extraordinary speculative breadth my friend retorted that there was no cad like your cultivated cad, and that I might depend upon discovering—since I had had the levity not already to have enquired—that my shining light proceeded, a generation back, from a Methodist cheesemonger. I confess I was struck with his insistence, and I said, after reflexion: "It may be—I admit it may be; but why on earth are you so sure?"—asking the question mainly to lay him the trap of saying that it was because the poor man didn't dress for dinner. He took an instant to circumvent my trap and come blandly out the other side.

"Because the Kent Mulvilles have invented him. They've an infallible hand for frauds. All their geese are swans. They were born to be duped, they like it, they cry for it, they don't know anything from anything, and they disgust one—luckily perhaps!—with Christian charity." His vehemence was doubtless an accident, but it might have been a strange foreknowledge. I forget what protest I dropped; it was at any rate something that led him to go on after a moment: "I only ask one thing—it's perfectly simple. Is a man, in a given case, a real gentleman?"

"A real gentleman, my dear fellow—that's so soon said!"

"Not so soon when he isn't! If they've got hold of one this time he must be a great rascal!"

"I might feel injured," I answered, "if I didn't reflect that they don't rave about me."

"Don't be too sure! I'll grant that he's a gentleman," Gravener presently added, "if you'll admit that he's a scamp."

"I don't know which to admire most, your logic or your benevolence."

My friend coloured at this, but he didn't change the subject. "Where did they pick him up?"

"I think they were struck with something he had published."

"I can fancy the dreary thing!"

"I believe they found out he had all sorts of worries and difficulties."

"That of course wasn't to be endured, so they jumped at the privilege of paying his debts!" I professed that I knew nothing about his debts, and I reminded my visitor that though the dear Mulvilles were angels they were neither idiots nor millionaires. What they mainly aimed at was reuniting Mr. Saltram to his wife. "I was expecting to hear he has basely abandoned her," Gravener went on, at this, "and I'm too glad you don't disappoint me."

I tried to recall exactly what Mrs. Mulville had told me. "He didn't leave her—no. It's she who has left him."

"Left him to us?" Gravener asked. "The monster—many thanks! I decline to take him."

"You'll hear more about him in spite of yourself. I can't, no, I really can't resist the impression that he's a big man." I was already mastering—to my shame perhaps be it said—just the tone my old friend least liked.

"It's doubtless only a trifle," he returned, "but you haven't happened to mention what his reputation's to rest on."

"Why on what I began by boring you with—his extraordinary mind."

"As exhibited in his writings?"

"Possibly in his writings, but certainly in his talk, which is far and away the richest I ever listened to."

"And what's it all about?"

"My dear fellow, don't ask me! About everything!" I pursued, reminding myself of poor Adelaide. "About his ideas of things," I then more charitably added. "You must have heard him to know what I mean—it's unlike anything that ever was heard." I coloured, I admit, I overcharged a little, for such a picture was an anticipation of Saltram's later development and still more of my fuller acquaintance with him. However, I really expressed, a little lyrically perhaps, my actual imagination of him when I proceeded to declare that, in a cloud of tradition, of legend, he might very well go down to posterity as the greatest of all great talkers. Before we parted George Gravener had wondered why such a row should be made about a chatterbox the more and why he should be pampered and pensioned. The greater the wind-bag the greater the calamity. Out of proportion to everything else on earth had come to be this wagging of the tongue. We were drenched with talk—our wretched age was dying of it. I differed from him here sincerely, only going so far as to concede, and gladly, that we were drenched with sound. It was not however the mere speakers who were killing us—it was the mere stammerers. Fine talk was as rare as it was refreshing—the gift of the gods themselves, the one starry spangle on the ragged cloak of humanity. How many men were there who rose to this privilege, of how many masters of conversation could he boast the acquaintance? Dying of talk?—why we were dying of the lack of it! Bad writing wasn't talk, as many people seemed to think, and even good wasn't always to be compared to it. From the best talk indeed the best writing had something to learn. I fancifully added that we too should peradventure be gilded by the legend, should be pointed at for having listened, for having actually heard. Gravener, who had glanced at his watch and discovered it was midnight, found to all this a retort beautifully characteristic of him.

"There's one little fact to be borne in mind in the presence equally of the best talk and of the worst." He looked, in saying this, as if he meant great things, and I was sure he could only mean once more that neither of them mattered if a man wasn't a real gentleman. Perhaps it was what he did mean; he deprived me however of the exultation of being right by putting the truth in a slightly different way. "The only thing that really counts for one's estimate of a person is his conduct." He had his watch still in his palm, and I reproached him with unfair play in having ascertained beforehand that it was now the hour at which I always gave in. My pleasantry so far failed to mollify him that he promptly added that to the rule he had just enunciated there was absolutely no exception.

"None whatever?"

"None whatever."

"Trust me then to try to be good at any price!" I laughed as I went with him to the door. "I declare I will be, if I have to be horrible!"

III

IF that first night was one of the liveliest, or at any rate was the freshest, of my exaltations, there was another, four years later, that was one of my great discomposures. Repetition, I well knew by this time, was the secret of Saltram's power to alienate, and of course one would never have seen him at his finest if one hadn't seen him in his remorses. They set in mainly at this season and were magnificent, elemental, orchestral. I was quite aware that one of these atmospheric disturbances was now due; but none the less, in our arduous attempt to set him on his feet as a lecturer, it was impossible not to feel that two failures were a large order, as we said, for a short course of five. This was the second time, and it was past nine o'clock; the audience, a muster unprecedented and really encouraging, had fortunately the attitude of blandness that might have been looked for in persons whom the promise of (if I'm not mistaken) An Analysis of Primary Ideas had drawn to the neighbourhood of Upper Baker Street. There was in those days in that region a petty lecture-hall to be secured on terms as moderate as the funds left at our disposal by the irrepressible question of the maintenance of five small Saltrams—I include the mother—and one large one. By the time the Saltrams, of different sizes, were all maintained we had pretty well poured out the oil that might have lubricated the machinery for enabling the most original of men to appear to maintain them.

It was I, the other time, who had been forced into the breach, standing up there for an odious lamplit moment to explain to half a dozen thin benches, where earnest brows were virtuously void of anything so cynical as a suspicion, that we couldn't so much as put a finger on Mr. Saltram. There was nothing to plead but that our scouts had been out from the early hours and that we were afraid that on one of his walks abroad—he took one, for meditation, whenever he was to address such a company—some accident had disabled or delayed him. The meditative walks were a fiction, for he never, that any one could discover, prepared anything but a magnificent prospectus; hence his circulars and programmes, of which I possess an almost complete collection, are the solemn ghosts of generations never born. I put the case, as it seemed to me, at the best; but I admit I had been angry, and Kent Mulville was shocked at my want of public optimism. This time therefore I left the excuses to his more practised patience, only relieving myself in response to a direct appeal from a young lady next whom, in the hall, I found myself sitting. My position was an accident, but if it had been calculated the reason would scarce have eluded an observer of the fact that no one else in the room had an approach to an appearance. Our philosopher's "tail" was deplorably limp. This visitor was the only person who looked at her ease, who had come a little in the spirit of adventure. She seemed to carry amusement in her handsome young head, and her presence spoke, a little mystifyingly, of a sudden extension of Saltram's sphere of influence. He was doing better than we hoped, and he had chosen such an occasion, of all occasions, to succumb to heaven knew which of his fond infirmities. The young lady produced an impression of auburn hair and black velvet, and had on her other hand a companion of obscurer type, presumably a waiting-maid. She herself might perhaps have been a foreign countess, and before she addressed me I had beguiled our sorry interval by finding in her a vague recall of the opening of some novel of Madame Sand. It didn't make her more fathomable to pass in a few minutes from this to the certitude that she was American; it simply engendered depressing reflexions as to the possible check to contributions from Boston. She asked me if, as a person apparently more initiated, I would recommend further waiting, and I answered that if she considered I was on my honour I would privately deprecate it. Perhaps she didn't; at any rate our talk took a turn that prolonged it till she became aware we were left almost alone. I presently ascertained she knew Mrs. Saltram, and this explained in a manner the miracle. The brotherhood of the friends of the husband was as nothing to the brotherhood, or perhaps I should say the sisterhood, of the friends of the wife. Like the Kent Mulvilles I belonged to both fraternities, and even better than they I think I had sounded the abyss of Mrs. Saltram's wrongs. She bored me to extinction, and I knew but too well how she had bored her husband; but there were those who stood by her, the most efficient of whom were indeed the handful of poor Saltram's backers. They did her liberal justice, whereas her mere patrons and partisans had nothing but hatred for our philosopher. I'm bound to say it was we, however—we of both camps, as it were—who had always done most for her.

I thought my young lady looked rich—I scarcely knew why; and I hoped she had put her hand in her pocket. I soon made her out, however, not at all a fine fanatic—she was but a generous, irresponsible enquirer. She had come to England to see her aunt, and it was at her aunt's she had met the dreary lady we had all so much on our mind. I saw she'd help to pass the time when she observed that it was a pity this lady wasn't intrinsically more interesting. That was refreshing, for it was an article of faith in Mrs. Saltram's circle—at least among those who scorned to know her horrid husband—that she was attractive on her merits. She was in truth most ordinary person, as Saltram himself would have been if he hadn't been a prodigy. The question of vulgarity had no application to him, but it was a measure his wife kept challenging you to apply. I hasten to add that the consequences of your doing so were no sufficient reason for his having left her to starve. "He doesn't seem to have much force of character," said my young lady; at which I laughed out so loud that my departing friends looked back at me over their shoulders as if I were making a joke of their discomfiture. My joke probably cost Saltram a subscription or two, but it helped me on with my interlocutress. "She says he drinks like a fish," she sociably continued, "and yet she allows that his mind's wonderfully clear." It was amusing to converse with a pretty girl who could talk of the clearness of Saltram's mind. I expected next to hear she had been assured he was awfully clever. I tried to tell her—I had it almost on my conscience—what was the proper way to regard him; an effort attended perhaps more than ever on this occasion with the usual effect of my feeling that I wasn't after all very sure of it. She had come to-night out of high curiosity—she had wanted to learn this proper way for herself. She had read some of his papers and hadn't understood them; but it was at home, at her aunt's, that her curiosity had been kindled—kindled mainly by his wife's remarkable stories of his want of virtue. "I suppose they ought to have kept me away," my companion dropped, "and I suppose they'd have done so if I hadn't somehow got an idea that he's fascinating. In fact Mrs. Saltram herself says he is."

"So you came to see where the fascination resides? Well, you've seen!"

My young lady raised fine eyebrows. "Do you mean in his bad faith?"

"In the extraordinary effects of it; his possession, that is, of some quality or other that condemns us in advance to forgive him the humiliation, as I may call it, to which he has subjected us."

"The humiliation?"

"Why mine, for instance, as one of his guarantors, before you as the purchaser of a ticket."

She let her charming gay eyes rest on me. "You don't look humiliated a bit, and if you did I should let you off, disappointed as I am; for the mysterious quality you speak of is just the quality I came to see."

"Oh, you can't 'see' it!" I cried.

"How then do you get at it?"

"You don't! You mustn't suppose he's good-looking," I added.

"Why his wife says he's lovely!"

My hilarity may have struck her as excessive, but I confess it broke out afresh. Had she acted only in obedience to this singular plea, so characteristic, on Mrs. Saltram's part, of what was irritating in the narrowness of that lady's point of view? "Mrs. Saltram," I explained, "undervalues him where he's strongest, so that, to make up for it perhaps, she overpraises him where he's weak. He's not, assuredly, superficially attractive; he's middle-aged, fat, featureless save for his great eyes."

"Yes, his great eyes," said my young lady attentively. She had evidently heard all about his great eyes—the beaux yeux for which alone we had really done it all.

"They're tragic and splendid—lights on a dangerous coast. But he moves badly and dresses worse, and altogether he's anything but smart."

My companion, who appeared to reflect on this, after a moment appealed. "Do you call him a real gentleman?"

I started slightly at the question, for I had a sense of recognising it: George Gravener, years before, that first flushed night, had put me face to face with it. It had embarrassed me then, but it didn't embarrass me now, for I had lived with it and overcome it and disposed of it. "A real gentleman? Emphatically not!"

My promptitude surprised her a little, but I quickly felt how little it was to Gravener I was now talking. "Do you say that because he's—what do you call it in England?—of humble extraction?"

"Not a bit. His father was a country school-master and his mother the widow of a sexton, but that has nothing to do with it. I say it simply because I know him well."

"But isn't it an awful drawback?"

"Awful—quite awful."

"I mean isn't it positively fatal?"

"Fatal to what? Not to his magnificent vitality."

Again she had a meditative moment. "And is his magnificent vitality the cause of his vices?"

"Your questions are formidable, but I'm glad you put them. I was thinking of his noble intellect. His vices, as you say, have been much exaggerated: they consist mainly after all in one comprehensive defect."

"A want of will?"

"A want of dignity."

"He doesn't recognise his obligations?"

"On the contrary, he recognises them with effusion, especially in public: he smiles and bows and beckons across the street to them. But when they pass over he turns away, and he speedily loses them in the crowd. The recognition's purely spiritual—it isn't in the least social. So he leaves all his belongings to other people to take care of. He accepts favours, loans, sacrifices—all with

nothing more deterrent than an agony of shame. Fortunately we're a littl
faithful band, and we do what we can." I held my tongue about the natura
children, engendered, to the number of three, in the wantonness of his youth
I only remarked that he did make efforts—often tremendous ones. "But th
efforts," I said, "never come to much: the only things that come to much ar
the abandonments, the surrenders."

"And how much do they come to?"

"You're right to put it as if we had a big bill to pay, but, as I've told you
before, your questions are rather terrible. They come, these mere exercise
of genius, to a great sum total of poetry, of philosophy, a mighty mass o
speculation, notation, quotation. The genius is there, you see, to meet th
surrender; but there's no genius to support the defence."

"But what is there, after all, at his age, to show?"

"In the way of achievement recognised and reputation established?"
asked. "To 'show' if you will, there isn't much, since his writing, mostly, isn'
as fine, isn't certainly as showy, as his talk. Moreover two-thirds of his worl
are merely colossal projects and announcements. 'Showing' Frank Saltram i
often a poor business," I went on: "we endeavoured, you'll have observed, t
show him to-night! However, if he had lectured he'd have lectured divinely
It would just have been his talk."

"And what would his talk just have been?"

I was conscious of some ineffectiveness, as well perhaps as of a littl
impatience, as I replied: "The exhibition of a splendid intellect." My young
lady looked not quite satisfied at this, but as I wasn't prepared for anothe
question I hastily pursued: "The sight of a great suspended swinging crystal—
huge lucid lustrous, a block of light—flashing back every impression of life
and every possibility of thought!"

This gave her something to turn over till we had passed out to the dusky
porch of the hall, in front of which the lamps of a quiet brougham were
almost the only thing Saltram's treachery hadn't extinguished. I went with
her to the door of her carriage, out of which she leaned a moment after she

had thanked me and taken her seat. Her smile even in the darkness was pretty. "I do want to see that crystal!"

"You've only to come to the next lecture."

"I go abroad in a day or two with my aunt."

"Wait over till next week," I suggested. "It's quite worth it."

She became grave. "Not unless he really comes!" At which the brougham started off, carrying her away too fast, fortunately for my manners, to allow me to exclaim "Ingratitude!"

IV

Mrs. Saltram made a great affair of her right to be informed where her husband had been the second evening he failed to meet his audience. She came to me to ascertain, but I couldn't satisfy her, for in spite of my ingenuity I remained in ignorance. It wasn't till much later that I found this had not been the case with Kent Mulville, whose hope for the best never twirled the thumbs of him more placidly than when he happened to know the worst. He had known it on the occasion I speak of—that is immediately after. He was impenetrable then, but ultimately confessed. What he confessed was more than I shall now venture to make public. It was of course familiar to me that Saltram was incapable of keeping the engagements which, after their separation, he had entered into with regard to his wife, a deeply wronged, justly resentful, quite irreproachable and insufferable person. She often appeared at my chambers to talk over his lapses; for if, as she declared, she had washed her hands of him, she had carefully preserved the water of this ablution, which she handed about for analysis. She had arts of her own of exciting one's impatience, the most infallible of which was perhaps her assumption that we were kind to her because we liked her. In reality her personal fall had been a sort of social rise—since I had seen the moment when, in our little conscientious circle, her desolation almost made her the fashion. Her voice was grating and her children ugly; moreover she hated the good Mulvilles, whom I more and more loved. They were the people who by doing most for her husband had in the long run done most for herself; and the warm confidence with which he had laid his length upon them was a pressure gentle compared with her stiffer persuadability. I'm bound to say he didn't criticise his benefactors, though practically he got tired of them; she, however, had the highest standards about eleemosynary forms. She offered the odd spectacle of a spirit puffed up by dependence, and indeed it had introduced her to some excellent society. She pitied me for not knowing certain people who aided her and whom she doubtless patronised in turn for their luck in not knowing me. I dare say I should have got on with her better if she had had a ray of imagination—if it had occasionally seemed to occur to her to regard Saltram's expressions of his nature in any other manner than as separate subjects of woe. They were all flowers of his character, pearls strung on an endless thread; but she had a stubborn little way of challenging them one after the other, as if she never suspected that he had a character, such as it was, or that deficiencies might be organic; the irritating effect of a mind incapable of a generalisation. One might doubtless have overdone the idea that there was a general licence for such a man; but if this had happened it would have been through one's feeling that there could be none for such a woman.

I recognised her superiority when I asked her about the aunt of the disappointed young lady: it sounded like a sentence from an English-French or other phrase-book. She triumphed in what she told me and she may have triumphed still more in what she withheld. My friend of the other evening, Miss Anvoy, had but lately come to England; Lady Coxon, the aunt, had been established here for years in consequence of her marriage with the late Sir Gregory of that name. She had a house in the Regent's Park, a Bath-chair and a fernery; and above all she had sympathy. Mrs. Saltram had made her acquaintance through mutual friends. This vagueness caused me to feel how much I was out of it and how large an independent circle Mrs. Saltram had at her command. I should have been glad to know more about the disappointed young lady, but I felt I should know most by not depriving her of her advantage, as she might have mysterious means of depriving me of my knowledge. For the present, moreover, this experience was stayed, Lady Coxon having in fact gone abroad accompanied by her niece. The niece, besides being immensely clever, was an heiress, Mrs. Saltram said; the only daughter and the light of the eyes of some great American merchant, a man, over there, of endless indulgences and dollars. She had pretty clothes and pretty manners, and she had, what was prettier still, the great thing of all. The great thing of all for Mrs. Saltram was always sympathy, and she spoke as if during the absence of these ladies she mightn't know where to turn for it. A few months later indeed, when they had come back, her tone perceptibly changed: she alluded to them, on my leading her up to it, rather as to persons in her debt for favours received. What had happened I didn't know, but I saw it would take only a little more or a little less to make her speak of them as thankless subjects of social countenance—people for whom she had vainly tried to do something. I confess I saw how it wouldn't be in a mere week or two that I should rid myself of the image of Ruth Anvoy, in whose very name, when I learnt it, I found something secretly to like. I should probably neither see her nor hear of her again: the knight's widow (he had been mayor of Clockborough) would pass away and the heiress would return to her inheritance. I gathered with surprise that she had not communicated to his wife the story of her attempt to hear Mr..Saltram, and I founded this reticence on the easy supposition that Mrs. Saltram had fatigued by overpressure the spring of the sympathy of which she boasted. The girl at any rate would forget the small adventure, be distracted, take a husband; besides which she would lack occasion to repeat her experiment.

We clung to the idea of the brilliant course, delivered without an accident, that, as a lecturer, would still make the paying public aware of our great man, but the fact remained that in the case of an inspiration so unequal there was treachery, there was fallacy at least, in the very conception of a series. In our scrutiny of ways and means we were inevitably subject to the old convention of the synopsis, the syllabus, partly of course not to lose the advantage of his grand free hand in drawing up such things; but for myself I laughed at our playbills even while I stickled for them. It was indeed amusing work to be scrupulous for Frank Saltram, who also at moments laughed about it, so far as the comfort of a sigh so unstudied as to be cheerful might pass for such a sound. He admitted with a candour all his own that he was in truth only to be depended on in the Mulvilles' drawing-room. "Yes," he suggestively allowed, "it's there, I think, that I'm at my best; quite late, when it gets toward eleven—and if I've not been too much worried." We all knew what too much worry meant; it meant too enslaved for the hour to the superstition of sobriety. On the Saturdays I used to bring my portmanteau, so as not to have to think of eleven o'clock trains. I had a bold theory that as regards this temple of talk and its altars of cushioned chintz, its pictures and its flowers, its large fireside and clear lamplight, we might really arrive at something if the Mulvilles would but charge for admission. Here it was, however, that they shamelessly broke down; as there's a flaw in every perfection this was the inexpugnable refuge of their egotism. They declined to make their saloon a market, so that Saltram's golden words continued the sole coin that rang there. It can have happened to no man, however, to be paid a greater price than such an enchanted hush as surrounded him on his greatest nights. The most profane, on these occasions, felt a presence; all minor eloquence grew dumb. Adelaide Mulville, for the pride of her hospitality, anxiously watched the door or stealthily poked the fire. I used to call it the music-room, for we had anticipated Bayreuth. The very gates of the kingdom of light seemed to open and the horizon of thought to flash with the beauty of a sunrise at sea.

In the consideration of ways and means, the sittings of our little board, we were always conscious of the creak of Mrs. Saltram's shoes. She hovered, she interrupted, she almost presided, the state of affairs being mostly such as to supply her with every incentive for enquiring what was to be done next. It was the pressing pursuit of this knowledge that, in concatenations of omnibuses and usually in very wet weather, led her so often to my door. She thought us spiritless creatures with editors and publishers; but she carried matters to no great effect when she personally pushed into back-shops. She wanted all moneys to be paid to herself: they were otherwise liable to such strange adventures. They trickled away into the desert—they were mainly at best, alas, a slender stream. The editors and the publishers were the last people to take this remarkable thinker at the valuation that has now pretty well come to be established. The former were half-distraught between the desire to "cut" him and the difficulty of finding a crevice for their shears; and when a volume on this or that portentous subject was proposed to the latter they suggested alternative titles which, as reported to our friend, brought into his face the noble blank melancholy that sometimes made it handsome. The title of an unwritten book didn't after all much matter, but some masterpiece of Saltram's may have died in his bosom of the shudder with which it was then convulsed. The ideal solution, failing the fee at Kent Mulville's door, would have been some system of subscription to projected treatises with their non-appearance provided for—provided for, I mean, by the indulgence of subscribers. The author's real misfortune was that subscribers were so wretchedly literal. When they tastelessly enquired why publication hadn't ensued I was tempted to ask who in the world had ever been so published. Nature herself had brought him out in voluminous form, and the money was simply a deposit on borrowing the work.

V

I WAS doubtless often a nuisance to my friends in those years; but there were sacrifices I declined to make, and I never passed the hat to George Gravener. I never forgot our little discussion in Ebury Street, and I think it stuck in my throat to have to treat him to the avowal I had found so easy to Mss Anvoy. It had cost me nothing to confide to this charming girl, but it would have cost me much to confide to the friend of my youth, that the character of the "real gentleman" wasn't an attribute of the man I took such pains for. Was this because I had already generalised to the point of perceiving that women are really the unfastidious sex? I knew at any rate that Gravener, already quite in view but still hungry and frugal, had naturally enough more ambition than charity. He had sharp aims for stray sovereigns being in view most from the tall steeple of Clockborough. His immediate ambition was to occupy à lui seul the field of vision of that smokily-seeing city and all his movements and postures were calculated for the favouring angle. The movement of the hand as to the pocket had thus to alternate gracefully with the posture of the hand on the heart. He talked to Clockborough in short only less beguilingly than Frank Saltram talked to his electors; with the difference to our credit, however, that we had already voted and that our candidate had no antagonist but himself. He had more than once been at Wimbledon—it was Mrs. Mulville's work not mine—and by the time the claret was served had seen the god descend. He took more pains to swing his censer than I had expected, but on our way back to town he forestalled any little triumph I might have been so artless as to express by the observation that such a man was—a hundred times!—a man to use and never a man to be used by. I remember that this neat remark humiliated me almost as much as if virtually, in the fever of broken slumbers, I hadn't often made it myself. The difference was that on Gravener's part a force attached to it that could never attach to it on mine. He was able to use people—he had the machinery; and the irony of Saltram's being made showy at Clockborough came out to me when he said, as if he had no memory of our original talk and the idea were quite fresh to him: "I hate his type, you know, but I'll be hanged if I don't put some of those things in. I can find a place for them: we might even find a place for the fellow himself." I myself should have had some fear—not, I need scarcely say, for the "things" themselves, but for some other things very near them; in fine for the rest of my eloquence.

Later on I could see that the oracle of Wimbledon was not in this case so appropriate as he would have been had the polities of the gods only coincided more exactly with those of the party. There was a distinct moment when, without saying anything more definite to me, Gravener entertained the idea of annexing Mr. Saltram. Such a project was delusive, for the discovery of analogies between his body of doctrine and that pressed from headquarters upon Clockborough—the bottling, in a word, of the air of those lungs for convenient public uncorking in corn-exchanges—was an experiment for which no one had the leisure. The only thing would have been to carry him massively about, paid, caged, clipped; to turn him on for a particular occasion in a particular channel. Frank Saltram's channel, however, was essentially not calculable, and there was no knowing what disastrous floods might have ensued. For what there would have been to do The Empire, the great newspaper, was there to look to; but it was no new misfortune that there were delicate situations in which The Empire broke down. In fine there was an instinctive apprehension that a clever young journalist commissioned to report on Mr. Saltram might never come back from the errand. No one knew better than George Gravener that that was a time when prompt returns counted double. If he therefore found our friend an exasperating waste of orthodoxy it was because of his being, as he said, poor Gravener, up in the clouds, not because he was down in the dust. The man would have been, just as he was, a real enough gentleman if he could have helped to put in a real gentleman. Gravener's great objection to the actual member was that he was not one.

Lady Coxon had a fine old house, a house with "grounds," at Clockborough, which she had let; but after she returned from abroad I learned from Mrs. Saltram that the lease had fallen in and that she had gone down to resume possession. I could see the faded red livery, the big square shoulders, the high-walled garden of this decent abode. As the rumble of dissolution grew louder the suitor would have pressed his suit, and I found myself hoping the politics of the late Mayor's widow wouldn't be such as to admonish her to ask him to dinner; perhaps indeed I went so far as to pray, they would naturally form a bar to any contact. I tried to focus the many-buttoned page, in the daily airing, as he perhaps even pushed the Bath-chair over somebody's toes. I was destined to hear, none the less, through Mrs. Saltram—who, I afterwards learned, was in correspondence with Lady Coxon's housekeeper— that Gravener was known to have spoken of the habitation I had in my eye as the pleasantest thing at Clockborough. On his part, I was sure, this was the voice not of envy but of experience. The vivid scene was now peopled, and I could see him in the old-time garden with Miss Anvoy, who would be certain, and very justly, to think him good-looking. It would be too much to describe myself as troubled by this play of surmise; but I occur to remember the relief, singular enough, of feeling it suddenly brushed away by an annoyance really much greater; an annoyance the result of its happening to come over me about that time with a rush that I was simply ashamed of Frank Saltram. There were limits after all, and my mark at last had been reached.

I had had my disgusts, if I may allow myself to-day such an expression; but this was a supreme revolt. Certain things cleared up in my mind, certain values stood out. It was all very well to have an unfortunate temperament; there was nothing so unfortunate as to have, for practical purposes, nothing else. I avoided George Gravener at this moment and reflected that at such a time I should do so most effectually by leaving England. I wanted to forget Frank Saltram—that was all. I didn't want to do anything in the world to him but that. Indignation had withered on the stalk, and I felt that one could pity him as much as one ought only by never thinking of him again. It wasn't for anything he had done to me; it was for what he had done to the Mulvilles. Adelaide cried about it for a week, and her husband, profiting by the example so signally given him of the fatal effect of a want of character, left the letter, the drop too much, unanswered. The letter, an incredible one, addressed by Saltram to Wimbledon during a stay with the Pudneys at Ramsgate, was the central feature of the incident, which, however, had many features, each more painful than whichever other we compared it with. The Pudneys had behaved shockingly, but that was no excuse. Base ingratitude, gross indecency—one had one's choice only of such formulas as that the more they fitted the less they gave one rest. These are dead aches now, and I am under no obligation, thank heaven, to be definite about the business. There are things which if I had had to tell them—well, would have stopped me off here altogether.

I went abroad for the general election, and if I don't know how much, on the Continent, I forgot, I at least know how much I missed, him. At a distance, in a foreign land, ignoring, abjuring, unlearning him, I discovered what he had done for me. I owed him, oh unmistakeably, certain noble conceptions; I had lighted my little taper at his smoky lamp, and lo it continued to twinkle. But the light it gave me just showed me how much more I wanted. I was pursued of course by letters from Mrs. Saltram which I didn't scruple not to read, though quite aware her embarrassments couldn't but be now of the gravest. I sacrificed to propriety by simply putting them away, and this is how, one day as my absence drew to an end, my eye, while I rummaged in my desk for another paper, was caught by a name on a leaf that had detached itself from the packet. The allusion was to Miss Anvoy, who, it appeared, was engaged to be married to Mr. George Gravener; and the news was two months old. A direct question of Mrs. Saltram's had thus remained unanswered—she had enquired of me in a postscript what sort of man this aspirant to such a hand might be. The great other fact about him just then was that he had been triumphantly returned for Clockborough in the interest of the party that had swept the country—so that I might easily have referred Mrs. Saltram to the journals of the day. Yet when I at last wrote her that I was coming home and would discharge my accumulated burden by seeing her, I but remarked in regard to her question that she must really put it to Miss Anvoy.

VI

I HAD almost avoided the general election, but some of its consequences, on my return, had smartly to be faced. The season, in London, began to breathe again and to flap its folded wings. Confidence, under the new Ministry, was understood to be reviving, and one of the symptoms, in a social body, was a recovery of appetite. People once more fed together, and it happened that, one Saturday night, at somebody's house, I fed with George Gravener. When the ladies left the room I moved up to where he sat and begged to congratulate him. "On my election?" he asked after a moment; so that I could feign, jocosely, not to have heard of that triumph and to be alluding to the rumour of a victory still more personal. I dare say I coloured however, for his political success had momentarily passed out of my mind. What was present to it was that he was to marry that beautiful girl; and yet his question made me conscious of some discomposure—I hadn't intended to put this before everything. He himself indeed ought gracefully to have done so, and I remember thinking the whole man was in this assumption that in expressing my sense of what he had won I had fixed my thoughts on his "seat." We straightened the matter out, and he was so much lighter in hand than I had lately seen him that his spirits might well have been fed from a twofold source. He was so good as to say that he hoped I should soon make the acquaintance of Miss Anvoy, who, with her aunt, was presently coming up to town. Lady Coxon, in the country, had been seriously unwell, and this had delayed their arrival. I told him I had heard the marriage would be a splendid one; on which, brightened and humanised by his luck, he laughed and said "Do you mean for her?" When I had again explained what I meant he went on: "Oh she's an American, but you'd scarcely know it; unless, perhaps," he added, "by her being used to more money than most girls in England, even the daughters of rich men. That wouldn't in the least do for a fellow like me, you know, if it wasn't for the great liberality of her father. He really has been most kind, and everything's quite satisfactory." He added that his eldest brother had taken a tremendous fancy to her and that during a recent visit at Coldfield she had nearly won over Lady Maddock. I gathered from something he dropped later on that the free-handed gentleman beyond the seas had not made a settlement, but had given a handsome present and was apparently to be looked to, across the water, for other favours. People are simplified alike by great contentments and great yearnings, and, whether or no it was Gravener's directness that begot my own, I seem to recall that in some turn taken by our talk he almost imposed it on me as an act of decorum to ask if Miss Anvoy had also by chance expectations from her aunt. My enquiry drew out that Lady Coxon, who was the oddest of women, would have in any contingency to act under her late husband's will, which was odder still, saddling her with a mass of queer obligations complicated with queer loopholes. There were several dreary people, Coxon cousins, old maids, to whom she would have more or less to minister. Gravener laughed, without saying no, when I suggested that the young lady might come in through a loophole; then suddenly, as if he suspected my turning a lantern on him, he declared quite dryly: "That's all rot—one's moved by other springs!"

A fortnight later, at Lady Coxon's own house, I understood well enough the springs one was moved by. Gravener had spoken of me there as an old friend, and I received a gracious invitation to dine. The Knight's widow was again indisposed—she had succumbed at the eleventh hour; so that I found Miss Anvoy bravely playing hostess without even Gravener's help, since, to make matters worse, he had just sent up word that the House, the insatiable House, with which he supposed he had contracted for easier terms, positively declined to release him. I was struck with the courage, the grace and gaiety of the young lady left thus to handle the fauna and flora of the Regent's Park. I did what I could to help her to classify them, after I had recovered from the confusion of seeing her slightly disconcerted at perceiving in the guest introduced by her intended the gentleman with whom she had had that talk about Frank Saltram. I had at this moment my first glimpse of the fact that she was a person who could carry a responsibility; but I leave the reader to judge of my sense of the aggravation, for either of us, of such a burden, when I heard the servant announce Mrs. Saltram. From what immediately passed between the two ladies I gathered that the latter had been sent for post-haste to fill the gap created by the absence of the mistress of the house. "Good!" I remember crying, "she'll be put by me;" and my apprehension was promptly justified. Mrs. Saltram taken in to dinner, and taken in as a consequence of an appeal to her amiability, was Mrs. Saltram with a vengeance. I asked myself what Miss Anvoy meant by doing such things, but the only answer I arrived at was that Gravener was verily fortunate. She hadn't happened to tell him of her visit to Upper Baker Street, but she'd certainly tell him to-morrow; not indeed that this would make him like any better her having had the innocence to invite such a person as Mrs. Saltram on such an occasion. It could only strike me that I had never seen a young woman put such ignorance into her cleverness, such freedom into her modesty; this, I think, was when, after dinner, she said to me frankly, with almost jubilant mirth: "Oh you don't admire Mrs. Saltram?" Why should I? This was truly a young person without guile. I had briefly to consider before I could reply that my objection to the lady named was the objection often uttered about people met at the social board—I knew all her stories. Then as Miss Anvoy remained momentarily vague I added: "Those about her husband."

"Oh yes, but there are some new ones."

"None for me. Ah novelty would be pleasant!"

"Doesn't it appear that of late he has been particularly horrid?"

"His fluctuations don't matter", I returned, "for at night all cats are grey. You saw the shade of this one the night we waited for him together. What will you have? He has no dignity."

Miss Anvoy, who had been introducing with her American distinctness looked encouragingly round at some of the combinations she had risked. "It too bad I can't see him."

"You mean Gravener won't let you?"

"I haven't asked him. He lets me do everything."

"But you know he knows him and wonders what some of us see in him."

"We haven't happened to talk of him," the girl said.

34

"Get him to take you some day out to see the Mulvilles."

"I thought Mr. Saltram had thrown the Mulvilles over."

"Utterly. But that won't prevent his being planted there again, to bloom like a rose, within a month or two."

Miss Anvoy thought a moment. Then, "I should like to see them," she said with her fostering smile.

"They're tremendously worth it. You mustn't miss them."

"I'll make George take me," she went on as Mrs. Saltram came up to interrupt us. She sniffed at this unfortunate as kindly as she had smiled at me and, addressing the question to her, continued: "But the chance of a lecture—one of the wonderful lectures? Isn't there another course announced?"

"Another? There are about thirty!" I exclaimed, turning away and feeling Mrs. Saltram's little eyes in my back. A few days after this I heard that Gravener's marriage was near at hand—was settled for Whitsuntide; but as no invitation had reached me I had my doubts, and there presently came to me in fact the report of a postponement. Something was the matter; what was the matter was supposed to be that Lady Coxon was now critically ill. I had called on her after my dinner in the Regent's Park, but I had neither seen her nor seen Miss Anvoy. I forget to-day the exact order in which, at this period, sundry incidents occurred and the particular stage at which it suddenly struck me, making me catch my breath a little, that the progression, the acceleration, was for all the world that of fine drama. This was probably rather late in the day, and the exact order doesn't signify. What had already occurred was some accident determining a more patient wait. George Gravener, whom I met again, in fact told me as much, but without signs of perturbation. Lady Coxon had to be constantly attended to, and there were other good reasons as well. Lady Coxon had to be so constantly attended to that on the occasion of a second attempt in the Regent's Park I equally failed to obtain a sight of her niece. I judged it discreet in all the conditions not to make a third; but this didn't matter, for it was through Adelaide Mulville that the side-wind of the comedy, though I was at first unwitting, began to reach me. I went to

35

Wimbledon at times because Saltram was there, and I went at others becaus
he wasn't. The Pudneys, who had taken him to Birmingham, had already go
rid of him, and we had a horrible consciousness of his wandering roofless, in
dishonour, about the smoky Midlands, almost as the injured Lear wandered
on the storm-lashed heath. His room, upstairs, had been lately done up (
could hear the crackle of the new chintz) and the difference only made hi
smirches and bruises, his splendid tainted genius, the more tragic. If he wasn'
barefoot in the mire he was sure to be unconventionally shod. These were the
things Adelaide and I, who were old enough friends to stare at each other in
silence, talked about when we didn't speak. When we spoke it was only abou
the brilliant girl George Gravener was to marry and whom he had brough
out the other Sunday. I could see that this presentation had been happy, fo
Mrs. Mulville commemorated it after her sole fashion of showing confidence
in a new relation. "She likes me—she likes me": her native humility exulted
in that measure of success. We all knew for ourselves how she liked those
who liked her, and as regards Ruth Anvoy she was more easily won over than
Lady Maddock.

VII

ONE of the consequences, for the Mulvilles, of the sacrifices they made for Frank Saltram was that they had to give up their carriage. Adelaide drove gently into London in a one-horse greenish thing, an early Victorian landau, hired, near at hand, imaginatively, from a broken-down jobmaster whose wife was in consumption—a vehicle that made people turn round all the more when her pensioner sat beside her in a soft white hat and a shawl, one of the dear woman's own. This was his position and I dare say his costume when on an afternoon in July she went to return Miss Anvoy's visit. The wheel of fate had now revolved, and amid silences deep and exhaustive, compunctions and condonations alike unutterable, Saltram was reinstated. Was it in pride or in penance that Mrs. Mulville had begun immediately to drive him about? If he was ashamed of his ingratitude she might have been ashamed of her forgiveness; but she was incorrigibly capable of liking him to be conspicuous in the landau while she was in shops or with her acquaintance. However, if he was in the pillory for twenty minutes in the Regent's Park—I mean at Lady Coxon's door while his companion paid her call—it wasn't to the further humiliation of any one concerned that she presently came out for him in person, not even to show either of them what a fool she was that she drew him in to be introduced to the bright young American. Her account of the introduction I had in its order, but before that, very late in the season, under Gravener's auspices, I met Miss Anvoy at tea at the House of Commons. The member for Clockborough had gathered a group of pretty ladies, and the Mulvilles were not of the party. On the great terrace, as I strolled off with her a little, the guest of honour immediately exclaimed to me: "I've seen him, you know—I've seen him!" She told me about Saltram's call.

"And how did you find him?"

"Oh so strange!"

"You didn't like him?"

"I can't tell till I see him again."

"You want to do that?"

She had a pause. "Immensely."

We went no further; I fancied she had become aware Gravener was looking at us. She turned back toward the knot of the others, and I said: "Dislike him as much as you will—I see you're bitten."

"Bitten?" I thought she coloured a little.

"Oh it doesn't matter!" I laughed; "one doesn't die of it."

"I hope I shan't die of anything before I've seen more of Mrs. Mulville." I rejoiced with her over plain Adelaide, whom she pronounced the loveliest woman she had met in England; but before we separated I remarked to her that it was an act of mere humanity to warn her that if she should see more of Frank Saltram—which would be likely to follow on any increase of acquaintance with Mrs. Mulville—she might find herself flattening her nose against the clear hard pane of an eternal question—that of the relative, that of the opposed, importances of virtue and brains. She replied that this was surely a subject on which one took everything for granted; whereupon I admitted that I had perhaps expressed myself ill. What I referred to was what I had referred to the night we met in Upper Baker Street—the relative importance (relative to virtue) of other gifts. She asked me if I called virtue a gift—a thing handed to us in a parcel on our first birthday; and I declared that this very enquiry proved to me the problem had already caught her by the skirt. She would have help however, the same help I myself had once had, in resisting its tendency to make one cross.

"What help do you mean?"

"That of the member for Clockborough."

She stared, smiled, then returned: "Why my idea has been to help him!"

She had helped him—I had his own word for it that at Clockborough her bedevilment of the voters had really put him in. She would do so doubtless again and again, though I heard the very next month that this fine faculty had undergone a temporary eclipse. News of the catastrophe first came to me from Mrs. Saltram, and it was afterwards confirmed at Wimbledon: poor Miss Anvoy was in trouble—great disasters in America had suddenly summoned her home. Her father, in New York, had suffered reverses, lost so much money that it was really vexatious as showing how much he had had. It was Adelaide who told me she had gone off alone at less than a week's notice.

"Alone? Gravener has permitted that?"

"What will you have? The House of Commons!"

I'm afraid I cursed the House of Commons: I was so much interested. Of course he'd follow her as soon as he was free to make her his wife; only she mightn't now be able to bring him anything like the marriage-portion of which he had begun by having the virtual promise. Mrs. Mulville let me know what was already said: she was charming, this American girl, but really these American fathers—! What was a man to do? Mr. Saltram, according to Mrs. Mulville, was of opinion that a man was never to suffer his relation to money to become a spiritual relation—he was to keep it exclusively material. "Moi pas comprendre!" I commented on this; in rejoinder to which Adelaide, with her beautiful sympathy, explained that she supposed he simply meant that the thing was to use it, don't you know? but not to think too much about it. "To take it, but not to thank you for it?" I still more profanely enquired. For a quarter of an hour afterwards she wouldn't look at me, but this didn't prevent my asking her what had been the result, that afternoon—in the Regent's Park, of her taking our friend to see Miss Anvoy.

"Oh so charming!" she answered, brightening. "He said he recognised in her a nature he could absolutely trust."

"Yes, but I'm speaking of the effect on herself."

Mrs. Mulville had to remount the stream. "It was everything one could wish."

Something in her tone made me laugh. "Do you mean she gave him—a dole?"

"Well, since you ask me!"

"Right there on the spot?"

Again poor Adelaide faltered. "It was to me of course she gave it."

I stared; somehow I couldn't see the scene. "Do you mean a sum of money?"

"It was very handsome." Now at last she met my eyes, though I could see it was with an effort. "Thirty pounds."

"Straight out of her pocket?"

"Out of the drawer of a table at which she had been writing. She just slipped the folded notes into my hand. He wasn't looking; it was while he was going back to the carriage." "Oh," said Adelaide reassuringly, "I take care of it for him!" The dear practical soul thought my agitation, for I confess I was agitated, referred to the employment of the money. Her disclosure made me for a moment muse violently, and I dare say that during that moment I wondered if anything else in the world makes people so gross as unselfishness. I uttered, I suppose, some vague synthetic cry, for she went on as if she had had a glimpse of my inward amaze at such passages. "I assure you, my dear friend, he was in one of his happy hours."

But I wasn't thinking of that. "Truly indeed these Americans!" I said. "With her father in the very act, as it were, of swindling her betrothed!"

Mrs. Mulville stared. "Oh I suppose Mr. Anvoy has scarcely gone bankrupt—or whatever he has done—on purpose. Very likely they won't be able to keep it up, but there it was, and it was a very beautiful impulse."

"You say Saltram was very fine?"

"Beyond everything. He surprised even me."

"And I know what you've enjoyed." After a moment I added: "Had he peradventure caught a glimpse of the money in the table-drawer?"

At this my companion honestly flushed. "How can you be so cruel when you know how little he calculates?"

40

"Forgive me, I do know it. But you tell me things that act on my nerves. I'm sure he hadn't caught a glimpse of anything but some splendid idea."

Mrs. Mulville brightly concurred. "And perhaps even of her beautiful listening face."

"Perhaps even! And what was it all about?"

"His talk? It was apropos of her engagement, which I had told him about: the idea of marriage, the philosophy, the poetry, the sublimity of it." It was impossible wholly to restrain one's mirth at this, and some rude ripple that I emitted again caused my companion to admonish me. "It sounds a little stale, but you know his freshness."

"Of illustration? Indeed I do!"

"And how he has always been right on that great question."

"On what great question, dear lady, hasn't he been right?"

"Of what other great men can you equally say so?—and that he has never, but never, had a deflexion?" Mrs. Mulville exultantly demanded.

I tried to think of some other great man, but I had to give it up. "Didn't Miss Anvoy express her satisfaction in any less diffident way than by her charming present?" I was reduced to asking instead.

"Oh yes, she overflowed to me on the steps while he was getting into the carriage." These words somehow brushed up a picture of Saltram's big shawled back as he hoisted himself into the green landau. "She said she wasn't disappointed," Adelaide pursued.

I turned it over. "Did he wear his shawl?"

"His shawl?" She hadn't even noticed.

"I mean yours."

"He looked very nice, and you know he's really clean. Miss Anvoy used such a remarkable expression—she said his mind's like a crystal!"

41

I pricked up my ears. "A crystal?"

"Suspended in the moral world—swinging and shining and flashing there. She's monstrously clever, you know."

I thought again. "Monstrously!"

VIII

GEORGE GRAVENER didn't follow her, for late in September, after the House had risen, I met him in a railway-carriage. He was coming up from Scotland and I had just quitted some relations who lived near Durham. The current of travel back to London wasn't yet strong; at any rate on entering the compartment I found he had had it for some time to himself. We fared in company, and though he had a blue-book in his lap and the open jaws of his bag threatened me with the white teeth of confused papers, we inevitably, we even at last sociably conversed. I saw things weren't well with him, but I asked no question till something dropped by himself made, as it had made on another occasion, an absence of curiosity invidious. He mentioned that he was worried about his good old friend Lady Coxon, who, with her niece likely to be detained some time in America, lay seriously ill at Clockborough, much on his mind and on his hands.

"Ah Miss Anvoy's in America?"

"Her father has got into horrid straits—has lost no end of money."

I waited, after expressing due concern, but I eventually said: "I hope that raises no objection to your marriage."

"None whatever; moreover it's my trade to meet objections. But it may create tiresome delays, of which there have been too many, from various causes, already. Lady Coxon got very bad, then she got much better. Then Mr. Anvoy suddenly began to totter, and now he seems quite on his back. I'm afraid he's really in for some big reverse. Lady Coxon's worse again, awfully upset by the news from America, and she sends me word that she *must* have Ruth. How can I supply her with Ruth? I haven't got Ruth myself!"

"Surely you haven't lost her?" I returned.

"She's everything to her wretched father. She writes me every post—telling me to smooth her aunt's pillow. I've other things to smooth; but the old lady, save for her servants, is really alone. She won't receive her Coxon relations—she's angry at so much of her money going to them. Besides, she's hopelessly mad," said Gravener very frankly.

I don't remember whether it was this, or what it was, that made me ask if she hadn't such an appreciation of Mrs. Saltram as might render that active person of some use.

He gave me a cold glance, wanting to know what had put Mrs. Saltram into my head, and I replied that she was unfortunately never out of it. I happened to remember the wonderful accounts she had given me of the kindness Lady Coxon had shown her. Gravener declared this to be false; Lady Coxon, who didn't care for her, hadn't seen her three times. The only foundation for it was that Miss Anvoy, who used, poor girl, to chuck money about in a manner she must now regret, had for an hour seen in the miserable woman—you could never know what she'd see in people—an interesting pretext for the liberality with which her nature overflowed. But even Miss Anvoy was now quite tired of her. Gravener told me more about the crash in New York and the annoyance it had been to him, and we also glanced here and there in other directions; but by the time we got to Doncaster the principal thing he had let me see was that he was keeping something back. We stopped at that station, and, at the carriage-door, some one made a movement to get in. Gravener uttered a sound of impatience, and I felt sure that but for this I should have had the secret. Then the intruder, for some reason, spared us his company; we started afresh, and my hope of a disclosure returned. My companion held his tongue, however, and I pretended to go to sleep; in fact I really dozed for discouragement. When I reopened my eyes he was looking at me with an injured air. He tossed away with some vivacity the remnant of a cigarette and then said: "If you're not too sleepy I want to put you a case." I answered that I'd make every effort to attend, and welcomed the note of interest when he went on: "As I told you a while ago, Lady Coxon, poor dear, is demented." His tone had much behind it—was full of promise. I asked if her ladyship's misfortune were a trait of her malady or only of her character, and he pronounced it a product of both. The case he wanted to put to me was a matter on which it concerned him to have the impression—the judgement, he might also say—of another person. "I mean of the average intelligent

44

man, but you see I take what I can get." There would be the technical, the strictly legal view; then there would be the way the question would strike a man of the world. He had lighted another cigarette while he talked, and I saw he was glad to have it to handle when he brought out at last, with a laugh slightly artificial: "In fact it's a subject on which Miss Anvoy and I are pulling different ways."

"And you want me to decide between you? I decide in advance for Miss Anvoy."

"In advance—that's quite right. That's how I decided when I proposed to her. But my story will interest you only so far as your mind isn't made up." Gravener puffed his cigarette a minute and then continued: "Are you familiar with the idea of the Endowment of Research?"

"Of Research?" I was at sea a moment.

"I give you Lady Coxon's phrase. She has it on the brain."

"She wishes to endow—?"

"Some earnest and 'loyal' seeker," Gravener said. "It was a sketchy design of her late husband's, and he handed it on to her; setting apart in his will a sum of money of which she was to enjoy the interest for life, but of which, should she eventually see her opportunity—the matter was left largely to her discretion—she would best honour his memory by determining the exemplary public use. This sum of money, no less than thirteen thousand pounds, was to be called The Coxon Fund; and poor Sir Gregory evidently proposed to himself that The Coxon Fund should cover his name with glory—be universally desired and admired. He left his wife a full declaration of his views, so far at least as that term may be applied to views vitiated by a vagueness really infantine. A little learning's a dangerous thing, and a good citizen who happens to have been an ass is worse for a community than bad sewerage. He's worst of all when he's dead, because then he can't be stopped. However, such as they were, the poor man's aspirations are now in his wife's bosom, or fermenting rather in her foolish brain: it lies with her to carry them out. But of course she must first catch her hare."

45

"Her earnest loyal seeker?"

"The flower that blushes unseen for want of such a pecuniary independence as may aid the light that's in it to shine upon the human race. The individual, in a word, who, having the rest of the machinery, the spiritual the intellectual, is most hampered in his search."

"His search for what?"

"For Moral Truth. That's what Sir Gregory calls it."

I burst out laughing. "Delightful munificent Sir Gregory! It's a charming idea."

"So Miss Anvoy thinks."

"Has she a candidate for the Fund?"

"Not that I know of—and she's perfectly reasonable about it. But Lady Coxon has put the matter before her, and we've naturally had a lot of talk."

"Talk that, as you've so interestingly intimated, has landed you in a disagreement."

"She considers there's something in it," Gravener said.

"And you consider there's nothing?"

"It seems to me a piece of solemn twaddle—which can't fail to be attended with consequences certainly grotesque and possibly immoral. To begin with fancy constituting an endowment without establishing a tribunal—a bench of competent people, of judges."

"The sole tribunal is Lady Coxon?"

"And any one she chooses to invite."

"But she has invited you," I noted.

"I'm not competent—I hate the thing. Besides, she hasn't," my friend went on. "The real history of the matter, I take it, is that the inspiration was originally Lady Coxon's own, that she infected him with it, and that the

46

flattering option left her is simply his tribute to her beautiful, her aboriginal enthusiasm. She came to England forty years ago, a thin transcendental Bostonian, and even her odd happy frumpy Clockborough marriage never really materialised her. She feels indeed that she has become very British—as if that, as a process, as a 'Werden,' as anything but an original sign of grace, were conceivable; but it's precisely what makes her cling to the notion of the 'Fund'—cling to it as to a link with the ideal."

"How can she cling if she's dying?"

"Do you mean how can she act in the matter?" Gravener asked. "That's precisely the question. She can't! As she has never yet caught her hare, never spied out her lucky impostor—how should she, with the life she has led?—her husband's intention has come very near lapsing. His idea, to do him justice, was that it *should* lapse if exactly the right person, the perfect mixture of genius and chill penury, should fail to turn up. Ah the poor dear woman's very particular—she says there must be no mistake."

I found all this quite thrilling—I took it in with avidity. "And if she dies without doing anything, what becomes of the money?" I demanded.

"It goes back to his family, if she hasn't made some other disposition of it."

"She may do that then—she may divert it?"

"Her hands are not tied. She has a grand discretion. The proof is that three months ago she offered to make the proceeds over to her niece."

"For Miss Anvoy's own use?"

"For Miss Anvoy's own use—on the occasion of her prospective marriage. She was discouraged—the earnest seeker required so earnest a search. She was afraid of making a mistake; every one she could think of seemed either not earnest enough or not poor enough. On the receipt of the first bad news about Mr. Anvoy's affairs she proposed to Ruth to make the sacrifice for her. As the situation in New York got worse she repeated her proposal."

"Which Miss Anvoy declined?"

"Except as a formal trust."

"You mean except as committing herself legally to place the money?"

"On the head of the deserving object, the great man frustrated," said Gravener. "She only consents to act in the spirit of Sir Gregory's scheme."

"And you blame her for that?" I asked with some intensity.

My tone couldn't have been harsh, but he coloured a little and there was a queer light in his eye. "My dear fellow, if I 'blamed' the young lady I'm engaged to I shouldn't immediately say it even to so old a friend as you." I saw that some deep discomfort, some restless desire to be sided with, reassuringly, approvingly mirrored, had been at the bottom of his drifting so far, and I was genuinely touched by his confidence. It was inconsistent with his habits; but being troubled about a woman was not, for him, a habit: that itself was an inconsistency. George Gravener could stand straight enough before any other combination of forces. It amused me to think that the combination he had succumbed to had an American accent, a transcendental aunt and an insolvent father; but all my old loyalty to him mustered to meet this unexpected hint that I could help him. I saw that I could from the insincere tone in which he pursued: "I've criticised her of course, I've contended with her, and it has been great fun." Yet it clearly couldn't have been such great fun as to make it improper for me presently to ask if Miss Anvoy had nothing at all settled on herself. To this he replied that she had only a trifle from her mother—a mere four hundred a year, which was exactly why it would be convenient to him that she shouldn't decline, in the face of this total change in her prospects, an accession of income which would distinctly help them to marry. When I enquired if there were no other way in which so rich and so affectionate an aunt could cause the weight of her benevolence to be felt, he answered that Lady Coxon was affectionate indeed, but was scarcely to be called rich. She could let her project of the Fund lapse for her niece's benefit, but she couldn't do anything else. She had been accustomed to regard her as tremendously provided for, and she was up to her eyes in promises to anxious Coxons. She was a woman of an inordinate conscience, and her conscience

48

was now a distress to her, hovering round her bed in irreconcilable forms of resentful husbands, portionless nieces and undiscoverable philosophers.

We were by this time getting into the whirr of fleeting platforms, the multiplication of lights. "I think you'll find," I said with a laugh, "that your predicament will disappear in the very fact that the philosopher *is* undiscoverable."

He began to gather up his papers. "Who can set a limit to the ingenuity of an extravagant woman?"

"Yes, after all, who indeed?" I echoed as I recalled the extravagance commemorated in Adelaide's anecdote of Miss Anvoy and the thirty pounds.

IX

THE thing I had been most sensible of in that talk with George Gravener was the way Saltram's name kept out of it. It seemed to me at the time that we were quite pointedly silent about him; but afterwards it appeared more probable there had been on my companion's part no conscious avoidance. Later on I was sure of this, and for the best of reasons—the simple reason of my perceiving more completely that, for evil as well as for good, he said nothing to Gravener's imagination. That honest man didn't fear him—he was too much disgusted with him. No more did I, doubtless, and for very much the same reason. I treated my friend's story as an absolute confidence; but when before Christmas, by Mrs. Saltram, I was informed of Lady Coxon's death without having had news of Miss Anvoy's return, I found myself taking for granted we should hear no more of these nuptials, in which, as obscurely unnatural, I now saw I had never *too* disconcertedly believed. began to ask myself how people who suited each other so little could please each other so much. The charm was some material charm, some afffinity, exquisite doubtless, yet superficial some surrender to youth and beauty and passion, to force and grace and fortune, happy accidents and easy contacts. They might dote on each other's persons, but how could they know each other's souls? How could they have the same prejudices, how could they have the same horizon? Such questions, I confess, seemed quenched but not answered when, one day in February, going out to Wimbledon, I found our young lady in the house. A passion that had brought her back across the wintry ocean was as much of a passion as was needed. No impulse equally strong indeed had drawn George Gravener to America; a circumstance on which, however, I reflected only long enough to remind myself that it was none of my business. Ruth Anvoy was distinctly different, and I felt that the difference was not simply that of her marks of mourning. Mrs. Mulville told me soon enough what it was: it was the difference between a handsome girl with large expectations and a handsome girl with only four hundred a year. This explanation indeed didn't wholly content me, not even when I learned that her mourning had a double cause—learned that poor Mr. Anvoy, giving way altogether, buried under the ruins of his fortune and leaving next to nothing, had died a few weeks before.

"So she has come out to marry George Gravener?" I commented. "Wouldn't it have been prettier of him to have saved her the trouble?"

"Hasn't the House just met?" Adelaide replied. "And for Mr. Gravener the House—!" Then she added: "I gather that her having come is exactly a sign that the marriage is a little shaky. If it were quite all right a self-respecting girl like Ruth would have waited for him over there."

I noted that they were already Ruth and Adelaide, but what I said was: "Do you mean she'll have had to return to *make* it so?"

"No, I mean that she must have come out for some reason independent of it." Adelaide could only surmise, however, as yet, and there was more, as we found, to be revealed. Mrs. Mulville, on hearing of her arrival, had brought the young lady out in the green landau for the Sunday. The Coxons were in possession of the house in Regent's Park, and Miss Anvoy was in dreary lodgings. George Gravener had been with her when Adelaide called, but had assented graciously enough to the little visit at Wimbledon. The carriage, with Mr. Saltram in it but not mentioned, had been sent off on some errand from which it was to return and pick the ladies up. Gravener had left them together, and at the end of an hour, on the Saturday afternoon, the party of three had driven out to Wimbledon. This was the girl's second glimpse of our great man, and I was interested in asking Mrs. Mulville if the impression made by the first appeared to have been confirmed. On her replying after consideration, that of course with time and opportunity it couldn't fail to be, but that she was disappointed, I was sufficiently struck with her use of this last word to question her further.

"Do you mean you're disappointed because you judge Miss Anvoy to be?"

"Yes; I hoped for a greater effect last evening. We had two or three people, but he scarcely opened his mouth."

"He'll be all the better to-night," I opined after a moment. Then I pursued: "What particular importance do you attach to the idea of her being impressed?"

Adelaide turned her mild pale eyes on me as for rebuke of my levity "Why the importance of her being as happy as *we* are!"

I'm afraid that at this my levity grew. "Oh that's a happiness almost too great to wish a person!" I saw she hadn't yet in her mind what I had in mine and at any rate the visitor's actual bliss was limited to a walk in the garden with Kent Mulville. Later in the afternoon I also took one, and I saw nothing of Miss Anvoy till dinner, at which we failed of the company of Saltram who had caused it to be reported that he was indisposed and lying down This made us, most of us—for there were other friends present—convey to each other in silence some of the unutterable things that in those years our eyes had inevitably acquired the art of expressing. If a fine little American enquirer hadn't been there we would have expressed them otherwise, and Adelaide would have pretended not to hear. I had seen her, before the very fact, abstract herself nobly; and I knew that more than once, to keep it from the servants, managing, dissimulating cleverly, she had helped her husband to carry him bodily to his room. Just recently he had been so wise and s deep and so high that I had begun to get nervous—to wonder if by chance there were something behind it, if he were kept straight for instance by the knowledge that the hated Pudneys would have more to tell us if they chose He was lying low, but unfortunately it was common wisdom with us in this connexion that the biggest splashes took place in the quietest pools. We should have had a merry life indeed if all the splashes had sprinkled us as refreshingly as the waters we were even then to feel about our ears. Kent Mulville had been up to his room, but had come back with a face that told as few tales as I had seen it succeed in telling on the evening I waited in the lecture-room with Miss Anvoy. I said to myself that our friend had gone out but it was a comfort that the presence of a comparative stranger deprived us of the dreary duty of suggesting to each other, in respect of his errand edifying possibilities in which we didn't ourselves believe. At ten o'clock he came into the drawing-room with his waistcoat much awry but his eye sending out great signals. It was precisely with his entrance that I ceased to be vividly conscious of him. I saw that the crystal, as I had called it, had begun to swing, and I had need of my immediate attention for Miss Anvoy.

Even when I was told afterwards that he had, as we might have said to-day, broken the record, the manner in which that attention had been rewarded relieved me of a sense of loss. I had of course a perfect general consciousness that something great was going on: it was a little like having been etherised to hear Herr Joachim play. The old music was in the air; I felt the strong pulse of thought, the sink and swell, the flight, the poise, the plunge; but I knew something about one of the listeners that nobody else knew, and Saltram's monologue could reach me only through that medium. To this hour I'm of no use when, as a witness, I'm appealed to—for they still absurdly contend about it—as to whether or no on that historic night he was drunk; and my position is slightly ridiculous, for I've never cared to tell them what it really was I was taken up with. What I got out of it is the only morsel of the total experience that is quite my own. The others were shared, but this is incommunicable. I feel that now, I'm bound to say, even in thus roughly evoking the occasion, and it takes something from my pride of clearness. However, I shall perhaps be as clear as is absolutely needful if I remark that our young lady was too much given up to her own intensity of observation to be sensible of mine. It was plainly not the question of her marriage that had brought her back. I greatly enjoyed this discovery and was sure that had that question alone been involved she would have stirred no step. In this case doubtless Gravener would, in spite of the House of Commons, have found means to rejoin her. It afterwards made me uncomfortable for her that, alone in the lodging Mrs. Mulville had put before me as dreary, she should have in any degree the air of waiting for her fate; so that I was presently relieved at hearing of her having gone to stay at Coldfield. If she was in England at all while the engagement stood the only proper place for her was under Lady Maddock's wing. Now that she was unfortunate and relatively poor, perhaps her prospective sister-in-law would be wholly won over.

There would be much to say, if I had space, about the way her behaviour, as I caught gleams of it, ministered to the image that had taken birth in my mind, to my private amusement, while that other night I listened to George Gravener in the railway-carriage. I watched her in the light of this queer possibility—a formidable thing certainly to meet—and I was aware that it coloured, extravagantly perhaps, my interpretation of her very looks and tones. At Wimbledon for instance it had appeared to me she was literally afraid of Saltram, in dread of a coercion that she had begun already to feel. I had come up to town with her the next day and had been convinced that, though deeply interested, she was immensely on her guard. She would show as little as possible before she should be ready to show everything. What this final exhibition might be on the part of a girl perceptibly so able to think things out I found it great sport to forecast. It would have been exciting to be approached by her, appealed to by her for advice; but I prayed to heaven I mightn't find myself in such a predicament. If there was really a present rigour in the situation of which Gravener had sketched for me the elements she would have to get out of her difficulty by herself. It wasn't I who had launched her and it wasn't I who could help her. I didn't fail to ask mysel why, since I couldn't help her, I should think so much about her. It was in part my suspense that was responsible for this; I waited impatiently to see whether she wouldn't have told Mrs. Mulville a portion at least of what I had learned from Gravener. But I saw Mrs. Mulville was still reduced to wonder what she had come out again for if she hadn't come as a conciliatory bride. That she had come in some other character was the only thing that fitted all the appearances. Having for family reasons to spend some time that spring in the west of England, I was in a manner out of earshot of the great oceanic rumble—I mean of the continuous hum of Saltram's thought—and my uneasiness tended to keep me quiet. There was something I wanted so little to have to say that my prudence surmounted my curiosity. I only wondered if Ruth Anvoy talked over the idea of The Coxon Fund with Lady Maddock and also somewhat why I didn't hear from Wimbledon. I had a reproachful note about something or other from Mrs. Saltram, but it contained no mention of Lady Coxon's niece, on whom her eyes had been much less fixed since the recent untoward events.

X

POOR Adelaide's silence was fully explained later—practically explained when in June, returning to London, I was honoured by this admirable woman with an early visit. As soon as she arrived I guessed everything, and as soon as she told me that darling Ruth had been in her house nearly a month I had my question ready. "What in the name of maidenly modesty is she staying in England for?"

"Because she loves me so!" cried Adelaide gaily. But she hadn't come to see me only to tell me Miss Anvoy loved her: that was quite sufficiently established, and what was much more to the point was that Mr. Gravener had now raised an objection to it. He had protested at least against her being at Wimbledon, where in the innocence of his heart he had originally brought her himself; he called on her to put an end to their engagement in the only proper, the only happy manner.

"And why in the world doesn't she do do?" I asked.

Adelaide had a pause. "She says you know."

Then on my also hesitating she added: "A condition he makes."

"The Coxon Fund?" I panted.

"He has mentioned to her his having told you about it."

"Ah but so little! Do you mean she has accepted the trust?"

"In the most splendid spirit—as a duty about which there can be no two opinions." To which my friend added: "Of course she's thinking of Mr. Saltram."

I gave a quick cry at this, which, in its violence, made my visitor turn pale. "How very awful!"

"Awful?"

"Why, to have anything to do with such an idea one's self."

"I'm sure *you* needn't!" and Mrs. Mulville tossed her head.

"He isn't good enough!" I went on; to which she opposed a sound almost as contentious as my own had been. This made me, with genuine immediate horror, exclaim: "You haven't influenced her, I hope!" and my emphasis brought back the blood with a rush to poor Adelaide's face. She declared while she blushed—for I had frightened her again—that she had never influenced anybody and that the girl had only seen and heard and judged for herself. *He* had influenced her, if I would, as he did every one who had a soul: that word, as we knew, even expressed feebly the power of the things he said to haunt the mind. How could she, Adelaide, help it if Miss Anvoy's mind was haunted? I demanded with a groan what right a pretty girl engaged to a rising M.P. had to *have* a mind; but the only explanation my bewildered friend could give me was that she was so clever. She regarded Mr. Saltram naturally as a tremendous force for good. She was intelligent enough to understand him and generous enough to admire.

"She's many things enough, but is she, among them, rich enough?" I demanded. "Rich enough, I mean, to sacrifice such a lot of good money?"

"That's for herself to judge. Besides, it's not her own money; she doesn't in the least consider it so."

"And Gravener does, if not *his* own; and that's the whole difficulty?"

"The difficulty that brought her back, yes: she had absolutely to see her poor aunt's solicitor. It's clear that by Lady Coxon's will she may have the money, but it's still clearer to her conscience that the original condition, definite, intensely implied on her uncle's part, is attached to the use of it. She can only take one view of it. It's for the Endowment or it's for nothing."

"The Endowment," I permitted myself to observe, "is a conception superficially sublime, but fundamentally ridiculous."

"Are you repeating Mr. Gravener's words?" Adelaide asked.

"Possibly, though I've not seen him for months. It's simply the way it strikes me too. It's an old wife's tale. Gravener made some reference to the legal aspect, but such an absurdly loose arrangement has *no* legal aspect."

"Ruth doesn't insist on that," said Mrs. Mulville; "and it's, for her, exactly this technical weakness that constitutes the force of the moral obligation."

"Are you repeating *her* words?" I enquired. I forget what else Adelaide said, but she said she was magnificent. I thought of George Gravener confronted with such magnificence as that, and I asked what could have made two such persons ever suppose they understood each other. Mrs. Mulville assured me the girl loved him as such a woman could love and that she suffered as such a woman could suffer. Nevertheless she wanted to see *me*. At this I sprang up with a groan. "Oh I'm so sorry!—when?" Small though her sense of humour, I think Adelaide laughed at my sequence. We discussed the day, the nearest it would be convenient I should come out; but before she went I asked my visitor how long she had been acquainted with these prodigies.

"For several weeks, but I was pledged to secrecy."

"And that's why you didn't write?"

"I couldn't very well tell you she was with me without telling you that no time had even yet been fixed for her marriage. And I couldn't very well tell you as much as that without telling you what I knew of the reason of it. It was not till a day or two ago," Mrs. Mulville went on, "that she asked me to ask you if you wouldn't come and see her. Then at last she spoke of your knowing about the idea of the Endowment."

I turned this over. "Why on earth does she want to see me?"

"To talk with you, naturally, about Mr. Saltram."

"As a subject for the prize?" This was hugely obvious, and I presently returned: "I think I'll sail to-morrow for Australia."

"Well then—sail!" said Mrs. Mulville, getting up.

But I frivolously, continued. "On Thursday at five, we said?" Th appointment was made definite and I enquired how, all this time, th unconscious candidate had carried himself.

"In perfection, really, by the happiest of chances: he has positively bee a dear. And then, as to what we revere him for, in the most wonderful form His very highest—pure celestial light. You *won't* do him an ill turn?" Adelaid pleaded at the door.

"What danger can equal for him the danger to which he's expose from himself?" I asked. "Look out sharp, if he has lately been too prim He'll presently take a day off, treat us to some exhibition that will make a Endowment a scandal."

"A scandal?" Mrs. Mulville dolorously echoed.

"Is Miss Anvoy prepared for that?"

My visitor, for a moment, screwed her parasol into my carpet. "H grows bigger every day."

"So do you!" I laughed as she went off.

That girl at Wimbledon, on the Thursday afternoon, more tha justified my apprehensions. I recognised fully now the cause of the agitatio she had produced in me from the first—the faint foreknowledge that ther was something very stiff I should have to do for her. I felt more than eve committed to my fate as, standing before her in the big drawing-room wher they had tactfully left us to ourselves, I tried with a smile to string togethe the pearls of lucidity which, from her chair, she successively tossed me. Pal and bright, in her monotonous mourning, she was an image of intelligen purpose, of the passion of duty; but I asked myself whether any girl ha ever had so charming an instinct as that which permitted her to laugh out as for the joy of her difficulty, into the priggish old room. This remarkabl young woman could be earnest without being solemn, and at moments whe I ought doubtless to have cursed her obstinacy I found myself watchin the unstudied play of her eyebrows or the recurrence of a singularly intens whiteness produced by the parting of her lips. These aberrations, I hasten to add, didn't prevent my learning soon enough why she had wished to see me. Her reason for this was as distinct as her beauty: it was to make me explain what I had meant, on the occasion of our first meeting, by Mr. Saltram's want of dignity. It wasn't that she couldn't imagine, but she desired it there from my lips. What she really desired of course was to know whether there was worse about him than what she had found out for herself. She hadn't been a month so much in the house with him without discovering that he wasn't a man of monumental bronze. He was like a jelly minus its mould, he had to be embanked; and that was precisely the source of her interest in him and the ground of her project. She put her project boldly before me: there it stood in its preposterous beauty. She was as willing to take the humorous view of it as I could be: the only difference was that for her the humorous view of a thing wasn't necessarily prohibitive, wasn't paralysing.

Moreover she professed that she couldn't discuss with me the primary question—the moral obligation: that was in her own breast. There were things she couldn't go into—injunctions, impressions she had received. They were a part of the closest intimacy of her intercourse with her aunt, they were absolutely clear to her; and on questions of delicacy, the interpretation of a fidelity, of a promise, one had always in the last resort to make up one's mind for one's self. It was the idea of the application to the particular case, such a splendid one at last, that troubled her, and she admitted that it stirred very deep things. She didn't pretend that such a responsibility was a simple matter; if it *had* been she wouldn't have attempted to saddle me with any portion of it. The Mulvilles were sympathy itself, but were they absolutely candid? Could they indeed be, in their position—would it even have been to be desired? Yes, she had sent for me to ask no less than that of me—whether there was anything dreadful kept back. She made no allusion whatever to George Gravener—I thought her silence the only good taste and her gaiety perhaps a part of the very anxiety of that discretion, the effect of a determination that people shouldn't know from herself that her relations with the man she was to marry were strained. All the weight, however, that she left me to throw was a sufficient implication of the weight *he* had thrown in vain. Oh she knew the question of character was immense, and that one

couldn't entertain any plan for making merit comfortable without running
the gauntlet of that terrible procession of interrogation-points which, like
a young ladies' school out for a walk, hooked their uniform noses at the
tail of governess Conduct. But were we absolutely to hold that there was
never, never, never an exception, never, never, never an occasion for liberal
acceptance, for clever charity, for suspended pedantry—for letting one side,
in short, outbalance another? When Miss Anvoy threw off this appeal I could
have embraced her for so delightfully emphasising her unlikeness to Mrs.
Saltram. "Why not have the courage of one's forgiveness," she asked, "as well
as the enthusiasm of one's adhesion?"

"Seeing how wonderfully you've threshed the whole thing out," I evasively
replied, "gives me an extraordinary notion of the point your enthusiasm has
reached."

She considered this remark an instant with her eyes on mine, and I
divined that it struck her I might possibly intend it as a reference to some
personal subjection to our fat philosopher, to some aberration of sensibility,
some perversion of taste. At least I couldn't interpret otherwise the sudden
flash that came into her face. Such a manifestation, as the result of any word
of mine, embarrassed me; but while I was thinking how to reassure her the
flush passed away in a smile of exquisite good nature. "Oh you see one
forgets so wonderfully how one dislikes him!" she said; and if her tone simply
extinguished his strange figure with the brush of its compassion, it also rings
in my ear to-day as the purest of all our praises. But with what quick response
of fine pity such a relegation of the man himself made me privately sigh
"Ah poor Saltram!" She instantly, with this, took the measure of all I didn't
believe, and it enabled her to go on: "What can one do when a person has
given such a lift to one's interest in life?"

"Yes, what can one do?" If I struck her as a little vague it was because I
was thinking of another person. I indulged in another inarticulate murmur—
"Poor George Gravener!" What had become of the lift *he* had given that
interest? Later on I made up my mind that she was sore and stricken at the
appearance he presented of wanting the miserable money. This was the hidden
reason of her alienation. The probable sincerity, in spite of the illiberality, of

his scruples about the particular use of it under discussion didn't efface the ugliness of his demand that they should buy a good house with it. Then, as for *his* alienation, he didn't, pardonably enough, grasp the lift Frank Saltram had given her interest in life. If a mere spectator could ask that last question, with what rage in his heart the man himself might! He wasn't, like her, I was to see, too proud to show me why he was disappointed.

XI

I was unable this time to stay to dinner: such at any rate was the plea on which I took leave. I desired in truth to get away from my young lady, for that obviously helped me not to pretend to satisfy her. How *could* I satisfy her? I asked myself—how could I tell her how much had been kept back? I didn't even know and I certainly didn't desire to know. My own policy had ever been to learn the least about poor Saltram's weaknesses—not to learn the most. A great deal that I had in fact learned had been forced upon me by his wife. There was something even irritating in Miss Anvoy's crude conscientiousness and I wondered why, after all, she couldn't have let him alone and been content to entrust George Gravener with the purchase of the good house. I was sure he would have driven a bargain, got something excellent and cheap. I laughed louder even than she, I temporised, I failed her; I told her I must think over her case. I professed a horror of responsibilities and twitted her with her own extravagant passion for them. It wasn't really that I was afraid of the scandal, the moral discredit for the Fund; what troubled me most was a feeling of a different order. Of course, as the beneficiary of the Fund was to enjoy a simple life-interest, as it was hoped that new beneficiaries would arise and come up to new standards, it wouldn't be a trifle that the first of these worthies shouldn't have been a striking example of the domestic virtues. The Fund would start badly, as it were, and the laurel would, in some respects at least, scarcely be greener from the brows of the original wearer. That idea however, was at that hour, as I have hinted, not the source of solicitude it ought perhaps to have been, for I felt less the irregularity of Saltram's getting the money than that of this exalted young woman's giving it up. I wanted her to have it for herself, and I told her so before I went away. She looked graver at this than she had looked at all, saying she hoped such a preference wouldn't make me dishonest.

It made me, to begin with, very restless—made me, instead of going straight to the station, fidget a little about that many-coloured Common which gives Wimbledon horizons. There was a worry for me to work off.

or rather keep at a distance, for I declined even to admit to myself that I had, in Miss Anvoy's phrase, been saddled with it. What could have been clearer indeed than the attitude of recognising perfectly what a world of trouble The Coxon Fund would in future save us, and of yet liking better to face a continuance of that trouble than see, and in fact contribute to, a deviation from attainable bliss in the life of two other persons in whom I was deeply interested? Suddenly, at the end of twenty minutes, there was projected across this clearness the image of a massive middle-aged man seated on a bench under a tree, with sad far-wandering eyes and plump white hands folded on the head of a stick—a stick I recognised, a stout gold-headed staff that I had given him in devoted days. I stopped short as he turned his face to me, and it happened that for some reason or other I took in as I had perhaps never done before the beauty of his rich blank gaze. It was charged with experience as the sky is charged with light, and I felt on the instant as if we had been overspanned and conjoined by the great arch of a bridge or the great dome of a temple. Doubtless I was rendered peculiarly sensitive to it by something in the way I had been giving him up and sinking him. While I met it I stood there smitten, and I felt myself responding to it with a sort of guilty grimace. This brought back his attention in a smile which expressed for me a cheerful weary patience, a bruised noble gentleness. I had told Miss Anvoy that he had no dignity, but what did he seem to me, all unbuttoned and fatigued as he waited for me to come up, if he didn't seem unconcerned with small things, didn't seem in short majestic? There was majesty in his mere unconsciousness of our little conferences and puzzlements over his maintenance and his reward.

After I had sat by him a few minutes I passed my arm over his big soft shoulder—wherever you touched him you found equally little firmness—and said in a tone of which the suppliance fell oddly on my own ear: "Come back to town with me, old friend—come back and spend the evening." I wanted to hold him, I wanted to keep him, and at Waterloo, an hour later, I telegraphed possessively to the Mulvilles. When he objected, as regards staying all night, that he had no things, I asked him if he hadn't everything of mine. I had abstained from ordering dinner, and it was too late for preliminaries at a club; so we were reduced to tea and fried fish at my rooms—reduced also to the transcendent. Something had come up which made me want him to feel at peace with me—and which, precisely, was all the dear man himself wanted on any occasion. I had too often had to press upon him considerations irrelevant but it gives me pleasure now to think that on that particular evening I didn't even mention Mrs. Saltram and the children. Late into the night we smoked and talked; old shames and old rigours fell away from us; I only let him see that I was conscious of what I owed him. He was as mild as contrition and as copious as faith; he was never so fine as on a shy return, and even better at forgiving than at being forgiven. I dare say it was a smaller matter than that famous night at Wimbledon, the night of the problematical sobriety and of Miss Anvoy's initiation; but I was as much in it on this occasion as I had been out of it then. At about 1.30 he was sublime.

He never, in whatever situation, rose till all other risings were over, and his breakfasts, at Wimbledon, had always been the principal reason mentioned by departing cooks. The coast was therefore clear for me to receive her when early the next morning, to my surprise, it was announced to me his wife had called. I hesitated, after she had come up, about telling her Saltram was in the house, but she herself settled the question, kept me reticent by drawing forth a sealed letter which, looking at me very hard in the eyes, she placed with a pregnant absence of comment, in my hand. For a single moment there glimmered before me the fond hope that Mrs. Saltram had tendered me, as it were, her resignation and desired to embody the act in an unsparing form. To bring this about I would have feigned any humiliation; but after my eyes had caught the superscription I heard myself say with a flatness that betrayed a sense of something very different from relief: "Oh the Pudneys!" I knew their envelopes though they didn't know mine. They always used the kind sold at post-offices with the stamp affixed, and as this letter hadn't been posted they had wasted a penny on me. I had seen their horrid missives to the Mulvilles but hadn't been in direct correspondence with them.

"They enclosed it to me, to be delivered. They doubtless explain to you that they hadn't your address."

I turned the thing over without opening it. "Why in the world should they write to me?"

64

"Because they've something to tell you. The worst," Mrs. Saltram dryly added.

It was another chapter, I felt, of the history of their lamentable quarrel with her husband, the episode in which, vindictively, disingenuously as they themselves had behaved, one had to admit that he had put himself more grossly in the wrong than at any moment of his life. He had begun by insulting the matchless Mulvilles for these more specious protectors, and then, according to his wont at the end of a few months, had dug a still deeper ditch for his aberration than the chasm left yawning behind. The chasm at Wimbledon was now blessedly closed; but the Pudneys, across their persistent gulf, kept up the nastiest fire. I never doubted they had a strong case, and I had been from the first for not defending him—reasoning that if they weren't contradicted they'd perhaps subside. This was above all what I wanted, and I so far prevailed that I did arrest the correspondence in time to save our little circle an infliction heavier than it perhaps would have borne. I knew, that is I divined, that their allegations had gone as yet only as far as their courage, conscious as they were in their own virtue of an exposed place in which Saltram could have planted a blow. It was a question with them whether a man who had himself so much to cover up would dare his blow; so that these vessels of rancour were in a manner afraid of each other. I judged that on the day the Pudneys should cease for some reason or other to be afraid they would treat us to some revelation more disconcerting than any of its predecessors. As I held Mrs. Saltram's letter in my hand it was distinctly communicated to me that the day had come—they had ceased to be afraid. "I don't want to know the worst," I presently declared.

"You'll have to open the letter. It also contains an enclosure."

I felt it—it was fat and uncanny. "Wheels within wheels!" I exclaimed. "There's something for me too to deliver."

"So they tell me—to Miss Anvoy."

I stared; I felt a certain thrill. "Why don't they send it to her directly?"

Mrs. Saltram hung fire. "Because she's staying with Mr. and Mrs. Mulville."

"And why should that prevent?"

Again my visitor faltered, and I began to reflect on the grotesque, the unconscious perversity of her action. I was the only person save George Gravener and the Mulvilles who was aware of Sir Gregory Coxon's and of Miss Anvoy's strange bounty. Where could there have been a more signal illustration of the clumsiness of human affairs than her having complacently selected this moment to fly in the face of it? "There's the chance of their seeing her letters. They know Mr. Pudney's hand."

Still I didn't understand; then it flashed upon me. "You mean they might intercept it? How can you imply anything so base?" I indignantly demanded.

"It's not I—it's Mr. Pudney!" cried Mrs. Saltram with a flush. "It's his own idea."

"Then why couldn't he send the letter to you to be delivered?"

Mrs. Saltram's embarrassment increased; she gave me another hard look "You must make that out for yourself."

I made it out quickly enough. "It's a denunciation?"

"A real lady doesn't betray her husband!" this virtuous woman exclaimed

I burst out laughing, and I fear my laugh may have had an effect of impertinence. "Especially to Miss Anvoy, who's so easily shocked? Why do such things concern *her*?" I asked, much at a loss.

"Because she's there, exposed to all his craft. Mr. and Mrs. Pudney have been watching this: they feel she may be taken in."

"Thank you for all the rest of us! What difference can it make when she has lost her power to contribute?"

Again Mrs. Saltram considered; then very nobly: "There are other things in the world than money." This hadn't occurred to her so long as the young lady had any; but she now added, with a glance at my letter, that Mr. and Mrs. Pudney doubtless explained their motives. "It's all in kindness," she continued as she got up.

66

"Kindness to Miss Anvoy? You took, on the whole, another view of kindness before her reverses."

My companion smiled with some acidity "Perhaps you're no safer than the Mulvilles!"

I didn't want her to think that, nor that she should report to the Pudneys that they had not been happy in their agent; and I well remember that this was the moment at which I began, with considerable emotion, to promise myself to enjoin upon Miss Anvoy never to open any letter that should come to her in one of those penny envelopes. My emotion, and I fear I must add my confusion, quickly deepened; I presently should have been as glad to frighten Mrs. Saltram as to think I might by some diplomacy restore the Pudneys to a quieter vigilance.

"It's best you should take *my* view of my safety," I at any rate soon responded. When I saw she didn't know what I meant by this I added: "You may turn out to have done, in bringing me this letter, a thing you'll profoundly regret." My tone had a significance which, I could see, did make her uneasy, and there was a moment, after I had made two or three more remarks of studiously bewildering effect, at which her eyes followed so hungrily the little flourish of the letter with which I emphasised them that I instinctively slipped Mr. Pudney's communication into my pocket. She looked, in her embarrassed annoyance, capable of grabbing it to send it back to him. I felt, after she had gone, as if I had almost given her my word I wouldn't deliver the enclosure. The passionate movement, at any rate, with which, in solitude, I transferred the whole thing, unopened, from my pocket to a drawer which I double-locked would have amounted, for an initiated observer, to some such pledge.

XII

Mrs. Saltram left me drawing my breath more quickly and indeed almost in pain—as if I had just perilously grazed the loss of something precious. I didn't quite know what it was—it had a shocking resemblance to my honour. The emotion was the livelier surely in that my pulses even yet vibrated to the pleasure with which, the night before, I had rallied to the rare analyst, the great intellectual adventurer and pathfinder. What had dropped from me like a cumbersome garment as Saltram appeared before me in the afternoon on the heath was the disposition to haggle over his value. Hang it, one had to choose, one had to put that value somewhere; so I would put it really high and have done with it. Mrs. Mulville drove in for him at a discreet hour—the earliest she could suppose him to have got up; and I learned that Miss Anvoy would also have come had she not been expecting a visit from Mr. Gravener. I was perfectly mindful that I was under bonds to see this young lady, and also that I had a letter to hand to her; but I took my time, I waited from day to day. I left Mrs. Saltram to deal as her apprehensions should prompt with the Pudneys. I knew at last what I meant—I had ceased to wince at my responsibility. I gave this supreme impression of Saltram time to fade if it would; but it didn't fade, and, individually, it hasn't faded even now. During the month that I thus invited myself to stiffen again, Adelaide Mulville, perplexed by my absence, wrote to me to ask why I *was* so stiff. At that season of the year I was usually oftener "with" them. She also wrote that she feared a real estrangement had set in between Mr. Gravener and her sweet young friend—a state of things but half satisfactory to her so long as the advantage resulting to Mr. Saltram failed to disengage itself from the merely nebulous state. She intimated that her sweet young friend was, if anything, a trifle too reserved; she also intimated that there might now be an opening for another clever young man. There never was the slightest opening, I may here parenthesise, and of course the question can't come up to-day. These are old frustrations now. Ruth Anvoy hasn't married, I hear, and neither have I. During the month, toward the end, I wrote to George Gravener to ask if, on a special errand, I might come to see him, and his answer was to knock the very next day at my door. I saw he had immediately connected my enquiry with the talk we had had in the railway-carriage, and his promptitude showed that the ashes of his eagerness weren't yet cold. I told him there was something I felt I ought in candour to let him know—I recognised the obligation his friendly confidence had laid on me.

"You mean Miss Anvoy has talked to you? She has told me so herself," he said.

"It wasn't to tell you so that I wanted to see you," I replied; "for it seemed to me that such a communication would rest wholly with herself. If however she did speak to you of our conversation she probably told you I was discouraging."

"Discouraging?"

"On the subject of a present application of The Coxon Fund."

"To the case of Mr. Saltram? My dear fellow, I don't know what you call discouraging!" Gravener cried.

"Well I thought I was, and I thought she thought I was."

"I believe she did, but such a thing's measured by the effect. She's not 'discouraged,'" he said.

"That's her own affair. The reason I asked you to see me was that it appeared to me I ought to tell you frankly that—decidedly!—I can't undertake to produce that effect. In fact I don't want to!"

"It's very good of you, damn you!" my visitor laughed, red and really grave. Then he said: "You'd like to see that scoundrel publicly glorified—perched on the pedestal of a great complimentary pension?"

I braced myself. "Taking one form of public recognition with another it seems to me on the whole I should be able to bear it. When I see the compliments that *are* paid right and left I ask myself why this one shouldn't take its course. This therefore is what you're entitled to have looked to me to mention to you. I've some evidence that perhaps would be really dissuasive but I propose to invite Mss Anvoy to remain in ignorance of it."

"And to invite me to do the same?"

"Oh you don't require it—you've evidence enough. I speak of a sealed letter that I've been requested to deliver to her."

"And you don't mean to?"

"There's only one consideration that would make me," I said.

Gravener's clear handsome eyes plunged into mine a minute, but evidently without fishing up a clue to this motive—a failure by which I was almost wounded. "What does the letter contain?"

"It's sealed, as I tell you, and I don't know what it contains."

"Why is it sent through you?"

"Rather than you?" I wondered how to put the thing. "The only explanation I can think of is that the person sending it may have imagined your relations with Miss Anvoy to be at an end—may have been told this is the case by Mrs. Saltram."

"My relations with Miss Anvoy are not at an end," poor Gravener stammered.

Again for an instant I thought. "The offer I propose to make you gives me the right to address you a question remarkably direct. Are you still engaged to Miss Anvoy?"

"No, I'm not," he slowly brought out. "But we're perfectly good friends."

"Such good friends that you'll again become prospective husband and wife if the obstacle in your path be removed?"

"Removed?" he anxiously repeated.

"If I send Miss Anvoy the letter I speak of she may give up her idea."

"Then for God's sake send it!"

"I'll do so if you're ready to assure me that her sacrifice would now presumably bring about your marriage."

"I'd marry her the next day!" my visitor cried.

"Yes, but would she marry *you*? What I ask of you of course is nothing less than your word of honour as to your conviction of this. If you give it me," I said, "I'll engage to hand her the letter before night."

Gravener took up his hat; turning it mechanically round he stood looking a moment hard at its unruffled perfection. Then very angrily honestly and gallantly, "Hand it to the devil!" he broke out; with which he clapped the hat on his head and left me.

"Will you read it or not?" I said to Ruth Anvoy, at Wimbledon, when I had told her the story of Mrs. Saltram's visit.

She debated for a time probably of the briefest, but long enough to make me nervous. "Have you brought it with you?"

"No indeed. It's at home, locked up."

There was another great silence, and then she said "Go back and destroy it."

I went back, but I didn't destroy it till after Saltram's death, when I burnt it unread. The Pudneys approached her again pressingly, but, prompt as they were, The Coxon Fund had already become an operative benefit and a general amaze: Mr. Saltram, while we gathered about, as it were, to watch the manna descend, had begun to draw the magnificent income. He drew it as he had always drawn everything, with a grand abstracted gesture. Its magnificence, alas, as all the world now knows, quite quenched him; it was the beginning of his decline. It was also naturally a new grievance for his wife, who began to believe in him as soon as he was blighted, and who at this hour accuses us of having bribed him, on the whim of a meddlesome American, to renounce his glorious office, to become, as she says, like everybody else. The very day he found himself able to publish he wholly ceased to produce. This deprived us, as may easily be imagined, of much of our occupation, and especially deprived the Mulvilles, whose want of self-support I never measured till they lost their great inmate. They've no one to live on now. Adelaide's most frequent reference to their destitution is embodied in the remark that dear far-away Ruth's intentions were doubtless good. She and Kent are even yet looking for another prop, but no one presents a true sphere of usefulness. They complain that people are self-sufficing. With Saltram the fine type of the child of adoption was scattered, the grander, the elder style. They've got their carriage back, but what's an empty carriage? In short I think we were all happier as well as poorer before; even including George Gravener, who by the deaths of his brother and his nephew has lately become Lord Maddock. His wife, whose fortune clears the property, is criminally dull; he hates being in the Upper House, and hasn't yet had high office. But what are these accidents, which I should perhaps apologise for mentioning, in the light of the great eventual boon promised the patient by the rate at which The Coxon Fund must be rolling up?

About Author

Henry James OM (15 April 1843 – 28 February 1916) was an American-British author regarded as a key transitional figure between literary realism and literary modernism, and is considered by many to be among the greatest novelists in the English language. He was the son of Henry James Sr. and the brother of renowned philosopher and psychologist William James and diarist Alice James.

He is best known for a number of novels dealing with the social and marital interplay between émigré Americans, English people, and continental Europeans. Examples of such novels include The Portrait of a Lady, The Ambassadors, and The Wings of the Dove. His later works were increasingly experimental. In describing the internal states of mind and social dynamics of his characters, James often made use of a style in which ambiguous or contradictory motives and impressions were overlaid or juxtaposed in the discussion of a character's psyche. For their unique ambiguity, as well as for other aspects of their composition, his late works have been compared to impressionist painting.

His novella The Turn of the Screw has garnered a reputation as the most analysed and ambiguous ghost story in the English language and remains his most widely adapted work in other media. He also wrote a number of other highly regarded ghost stories and is considered one of the greatest masters of the field.

James published articles and books of criticism, travel, biography, autobiography, and plays. Born in the United States, James largely relocated to Europe as a young man and eventually settled in England, becoming a British subject in 1915, one year before his death. James was nominated for the Nobel Prize in Literature in 1911, 1912 and 1916.

Life

Early years, 1843–1883

James was born at 2 Washington Place in New York City on 15 Apr 1843. His parents were Mary Walsh and Henry James Sr. His father wa intelligent and steadfastly congenial. He was a lecturer and philosopher wh had inherited independent means from his father, an Albany banker an investor. Mary came from a wealthy family long settled in New York Cit Her sister Katherine lived with her adult family for an extended period of time. Henry Jr. had three brothers, William, who was one year his senior, an younger brothers Wilkinson (Wilkie) and Robertson. His younger sister wa Alice. Both of his parents were of Irish and Scottish descent.

The family first lived in Albany, at 70 N. Pearl St., and then moved t Fourteenth Street in New York City when James was still a young boy. H education was calculated by his father to expose him to many influence primarily scientific and philosophical; it was described by Percy Lubbock, th editor of his selected letters, as "extraordinarily haphazard and promiscuous. James did not share the usual education in Latin and Greek classics. Betwee 1855 and 1860, the James' household traveled to London, Paris, Genev Boulogne-sur-Mer and Newport, Rhode Island, according to the father current interests and publishing ventures, retreating to the United State when funds were low. Henry studied primarily with tutors and briefl attended schools while the family traveled in Europe. Their longest stays wer in France, where Henry began to feel at home and became fluent in French He was afflicted with a stutter, which seems to have manifested itself onl when he spoke English; in French, he did not stutter.

In 1860 the family returned to Newport. There Henry became a frien of the painter John La Farge, who introduced him to French literature, an in particular, to Balzac. James later called Balzac his "greatest master," an said that he had learned more about the craft of fiction from him than from anyone else.

In the autumn of 1861 Henry received an injury, probably to his back while fighting a fire. This injury, which resurfaced at times throughout hi life, made him unfit for military service in the American Civil War.

In 1864 the James family moved to Boston, Massachusetts to be near William, who had enrolled first in the Lawrence Scientific School at Harvard and then in the medical school. In 1862 Henry attended Harvard Law School, but realised that he was not interested in studying law. He pursued his interest in literature and associated with authors and critics William Dean Howells and Charles Eliot Norton in Boston and Cambridge, formed lifelong friendships with Oliver Wendell Holmes Jr., the future Supreme Court Justice, and with James and Annie Fields, his first professional mentors.

His first published work was a review of a stage performance, "Miss Maggie Mitchell in Fanchon the Cricket," published in 1863. About a year later, A Tragedy of Error, his first short story, was published anonymously. James's first payment was for an appreciation of Sir Walter Scott's novels, written for the North American Review. He wrote fiction and non-fiction pieces for The Nation and Atlantic Monthly, where Fields was editor. In 1871 he published his first novel, Watch and Ward, in serial form in the Atlantic Monthly. The novel was later published in book form in 1878.

During a 14-month trip through Europe in 1869–70 he met Ruskin, Dickens, Matthew Arnold, William Morris, and George Eliot. Rome impressed him profoundly. "Here I am then in the Eternal City," he wrote to his brother William. "At last—for the first time—I live!" He attempted to support himself as a freelance writer in Rome, then secured a position as Paris correspondent for the New York Tribune, through the influence of its editor John Hay. When these efforts failed he returned to New York City. During 1874 and 1875 he published Transatlantic Sketches, A Passionate Pilgrim, and Roderick Hudson. During this early period in his career he was influenced by Nathaniel Hawthorne.

In 1869 he settled in London. There he established relationships with Macmillan and other publishers, who paid for serial installments that they would later publish in book form. The audience for these serialized novels was largely made up of middle-class women, and James struggled to fashion serious literary work within the strictures imposed by editors' and publishers' notions of what was suitable for young women to read. He lived in rented rooms but was able to join gentlemen's clubs that had libraries and where he could entertain male friends. He was introduced to English society by Henry Adams and Charles Milnes Gaskell, the latter introducing him to the Travellers' and the Reform Clubs.

In the fall of 1875 he moved to the Latin Quarter of Paris. Aside from two trips to America, he spent the next three decades—the rest of his life—in Europe. In Paris he met Zola, Alphonse Daudet, Maupassant, Turgenev, and others. He stayed in Paris only a year before moving to London.

In England he met the leading figures of politics and culture. He continued to be a prolific writer, producing The American (1877), The Europeans (1878), a revision of Watch and Ward (1878), French Poets and Novelists (1878), Hawthorne (1879), and several shorter works of fiction. In 1878 Daisy Miller established his fame on both sides of the Atlantic. It drew notice perhaps mostly because it depicted a woman whose behavior is outside the social norms of Europe. He also began his first masterpiece, The Portrait of a Lady, which would appear in 1881.

In 1877 he first visited Wenlock Abbey in Shropshire, home of his friend Charles Milnes Gaskell whom he had met through Henry Adams. He was much inspired by the darkly romantic Abbey and the surrounding countryside, which features in his essay Abbeys and Castles. In particular the gloomy monastic fishponds behind the Abbey are said to have inspired the lake in The Turn of the Screw.

While living in London, James continued to follow the careers of the "French realists", Émile Zola in particular. Their stylistic methods influenced his own work in the years to come. Hawthorne's influence on him faded during this period, replaced by George Eliot and Ivan Turgenev. 1879–1882 saw the publication of The Europeans, Washington Square, Confidence, and The Portrait of a Lady. He visited America in 1882–1883, then returned to London.

The period from 1881 to 1883 was marked by several losses. His mother died in 1881, followed by his father a few months later, and then by his brother Wilkie. Emerson, an old family friend, died in 1882. His friend Turgenev died in 1883.

Middle years, 1884–1897

In 1884 James made another visit to Paris. There he met again with Zola, Daudet, and Goncourt. He had been following the careers of the French "realist" or "naturalist" writers, and was increasingly influenced by them. In 1886, he published The Bostonians and The Princess Casamassima, both influenced by the French writers he'd studied assiduously. Critical reaction and sales were poor. He wrote to Howells that the books had hurt his career rather than helped because they had "reduced the desire, and demand, for my productions to zero". During this time he became friends with Robert Louis Stevenson, John Singer Sargent, Edmund Gosse, George du Maurier, Paul Bourget, and Constance Fenimore Woolson. His third novel from the 1880s was The Tragic Muse. Although he was following the precepts of Zola in his novels of the '80s, their tone and attitude are closer to the fiction of Alphonse Daudet. The lack of critical and financial success for his novels during this period led him to try writing for the theatre. (His dramatic works and his experiences with theatre are discussed below.)

In the last quarter of 1889, he started translating "for pure and copious lucre" Port Tarascon, the third volume of Alphonse Daudet adventures of Tartarin de Tarascon. Serialized in Harper's Monthly Magazine from June 1890, this translation praised as "clever" by The Spectator was published in January 1891 by Sampson Low, Marston, Searle & Rivington.

After the stage failure of Guy Domville in 1895, James was near despair and thoughts of death plagued him. The years spent on dramatic works were not entirely a loss. As he moved into the last phase of his career he found ways to adapt dramatic techniques into the novel form.

In the late 1880s and throughout the 1890s James made several trips through Europe. He spent a long stay in Italy in 1887. In that year the short novel The Aspern Papers and The Reverberator were published.

Late years, 1898–1916

In 1897–1898 he moved to Rye, Sussex, and wrote The Turn of the Screw. 1899–1900 saw the publication of The Awkward Age and The Sacred

Fount. During 1902–1904 he wrote The Ambassadors, The Wings of the Dove, and The Golden Bowl.

In 1904 he revisited America and lectured on Balzac. In 1906–1910 he published The American Scene and edited the "New York Edition", a 24-volume collection of his works. In 1910 his brother William died; Henry had just joined William from an unsuccessful search for relief in Europe on what then turned out to be his (Henry's) last visit to the United States (from summer 1910 to July 1911), and was near him, according to a letter he wrote, when he died.

In 1913 he wrote his autobiographies, A Small Boy and Others, and Notes of a Son and Brother. After the outbreak of the First World War in 1914 he did war work. In 1915 he became a British subject and was awarded the Order of Merit the following year. He died on 28 February 1916, in Chelsea, London. As he requested, his ashes were buried in Cambridge Cemetery in Massachusetts.

Biographers

James regularly rejected suggestions that he should marry, and after settling in London proclaimed himself "a bachelor". F. W. Dupee, in several volumes on the James family, originated the theory that he had been in love with his cousin Mary ("Minnie") Temple, but that a neurotic fear of sex kept him from admitting such affections: "James's invalidism ... was itself the symptom of some fear of or scruple against sexual love on his part." Dupee used an episode from James's memoir A Small Boy and Others, recounting a dream of a Napoleonic image in the Louvre, to exemplify James's romanticism about Europe, a Napoleonic fantasy into which he fled.

Dupee had not had access to the James family papers and worked principally from James's published memoir of his older brother, William, and the limited collection of letters edited by Percy Lubbock, heavily weighted toward James's last years. His account therefore moved directly from James's childhood, when he trailed after his older brother, to elderly invalidism. As more material became available to scholars, including the diaries of contemporaries and hundreds of affectionate and sometimes erotic letters written by James to younger men, the picture of neurotic celibacy gave way to a portrait of a closeted homosexual.

Between 1953 and 1972, Leon Edel authored a major five-volume biography of James, which accessed unpublished letters and documents after Edel gained the permission of James's family. Edel's portrayal of James included the suggestion he was celibate. It was a view first propounded by critic Saul Rosenzweig in 1943. In 1996 Sheldon M. Novick published Henry James: The Young Master, followed by Henry James: The Mature Master (2007). The first book "caused something of an uproar in Jamesian circles" as it challenged the previous received notion of celibacy, a once-familiar paradigm in biographies of homosexuals when direct evidence was non-existent. Novick also criticised Edel for following the discounted Freudian interpretation of homosexuality "as a kind of failure." The difference of opinion erupted in a series of exchanges between Edel and Novick which were published by the online magazine Slate, with the latter arguing that even the suggestion of celibacy went against James's own injunction "live!"—not "fantasize!"

A letter James wrote in old age to Hugh Walpole has been cited as an explicit statement of this. Walpole confessed to him of indulging in "high jinks", and James wrote a reply endorsing it: "We must know, as much as possible, in our beautiful art, yours & mine, what we are talking about — & the only way to know it is to have lived & loved & cursed & floundered & enjoyed & suffered — I don't think I regret a single 'excess' of my responsive youth".

The interpretation of James as living a less austere emotional life has been subsequently explored by other scholars. The often intense politics of Jamesian scholarship has also been the subject of studies. Author Colm Tóibín has said that Eve Kosofsky Sedgwick's Epistemology of the Closet made a landmark difference to Jamesian scholarship by arguing that he be read as a homosexual writer whose desire to keep his sexuality a secret shaped his layered style and dramatic artistry. According to Tóibín such a reading "removed James from the realm of dead white males who wrote about posh people. He became our contemporary."

James's letters to expatriate American sculptor Hendrik Christian Andersen have attracted particular attention. James met the 27-year-old Andersen in Rome in 1899, when James was 56, and wrote letters to Andersen that are intensely emotional: "I hold you, dearest boy, in my innermost love, & count on your feeling me—in every throb of your soul". In a letter of 6 May 1904, to his brother William, James referred to himself as "always your hopelessly celibate even though sexagenarian Henry". How accurate that description might have been is the subject of contention among James's biographers,   but the letters to Andersen were occasionally quasi-erotic: "I put, my dear boy, my arm around you, & feel the pulsation, thereby, as it were, of our excellent future & your admirable endowment." To his homosexual friend Howard Sturgis, James could write: "I repeat, almost to indiscretion, that I could live with you. Meanwhile I can only try to live without you."

His numerous letters to the many young gay men among his close male friends are more forthcoming. In a letter to Howard Sturgis, following a long visit, James refers jocularly to their "happy little congress of two" and in letters to Hugh Walpole he pursues convoluted jokes and puns about their relationship, referring to himself as an elephant who "paws you oh so benevolently" and winds about Walpole his "well meaning old trunk". His letters to Walter Berry printed by the Black Sun Press have long been celebrated for their lightly veiled eroticism.

He corresponded in almost equally extravagant language with his many female friends, writing, for example, to fellow novelist Lucy Clifford: "Dearest Lucy! What shall I say? when I love you so very, very much, and see you nine times for once that I see Others! Therefore I think that—if you want it made clear to the meanest intelligence—I love you more than I love Others." To his New York friend Mary Cadwalader Jones: "Dearest Mary Cadwalader I yearn over you, but I yearn in vain; & your long silence really breaks my heart, mystifies, depresses, almost alarms me, to the point even of making me wonder if poor unconscious & doting old Célimare [Jones's pet name for James] has 'done' anything, in some dark somnambulism of the spirit, which has ... given you a bad moment, or a wrong impression, or a 'colourable pretext' ... However these things may be, he loves you as tenderly as ever nothing, to the end of time, will ever detach him from you, & he remembers those Eleventh St. matutinal intimes hours, those telephonic matinées, as the most romantic of his life ..." His long friendship with American novelist Constance Fenimore Woolson, in whose house he lived for a number of weeks in Italy in 1887, and his shock and grief over her suicide in 1894, are discussed in detail in Edel's biography and play a central role in a study by Lyndall Gordon. (Edel conjectured that Woolson was in love with James and killed herself in part because of his coldness, but Woolson's biographers have objected to Edel's account.)

Works

Style and themes

James is one of the major figures of trans-Atlantic literature. His works frequently juxtapose characters from the Old World (Europe), embodying a feudal civilisation that is beautiful, often corrupt, and alluring, and from the New World (United States), where people are often brash, open, and assertive and embody the virtues—freedom and a more highly evolved moral character—of the new American society. James explores this clash of personalities and cultures, in stories of personal relationships in which power is exercised well or badly. His protagonists were often young American women facing oppression or abuse, and as his secretary Theodora Bosanquet remarked in her monograph Henry James at Work:

> When he walked out of the refuge of his study and into the world and looked around him, he saw a place of torment, where creatures of prey perpetually thrust their claws into the quivering flesh of doomed, defenseless children of light ... His novels are a repeated exposure of this wickedness, a reiterated and passionate plea for the fullest freedom of development, unimperiled by reckless and barbarous stupidity.

Critics have jokingly described three phases in the development of James's prose: "James I, James II, and The Old Pretender." He wrote short stories and plays. Finally, in his third and last period he returned to the long, serialised novel. Beginning in the second period, but most noticeably in the third, he increasingly abandoned direct statement in favour of frequent

83

double negatives, and complex descriptive imagery. Single paragraphs began to run for page after page, in which an initial noun would be succeeded by pronouns surrounded by clouds of adjectives and prepositional clauses, far from their original referents, and verbs would be deferred and then preceded by a series of adverbs. The overall effect could be a vivid evocation of a scene as perceived by a sensitive observer. It has been debated whether this change of style was engendered by James's shifting from writing to dictating to a typist, a change made during the composition of What Maisie Knew.

In its intense focus on the consciousness of his major characters, James's later work foreshadows extensive developments in 20th century fiction. Indeed, he might have influenced stream-of-consciousness writers such as Virginia Woolf, who not only read some of his novels but also wrote essays about them. Both contemporary and modern readers have found the late style difficult and unnecessary; his friend Edith Wharton, who admired him greatly, said that there were passages in his work that were all but incomprehensible. James was harshly portrayed by H. G. Wells as a hippopotamus laboriously attempting to pick up a pea that had got into a corner of its cage. The "late James" style was ably parodied by Max Beerbohm in "The Mote in the Middle Distance".

More important for his work overall may have been his position as an expatriate, and in other ways an outsider, living in Europe. While he came from middle-class and provincial beginnings (seen from the perspective of European polite society) he worked very hard to gain access to all levels of society, and the settings of his fiction range from working class to aristocratic, and often describe the efforts of middle-class Americans to make their way in European capitals. He confessed he got some of his best story ideas from gossip at the dinner table or at country house weekends. He worked for a living, however, and lacked the experiences of select schools, university, and army service, the common bonds of masculine society. He was furthermore a man whose tastes and interests were, according to the prevailing standards of Victorian era Anglo-American culture, rather feminine, and who was shadowed by the cloud of prejudice that then and later accompanied suspicions of his homosexuality. Edmund Wilson famously compared James's objectivity to Shakespeare's:

One would be in a position to appreciate James better if one compared him with the dramatists of the seventeenth century—Racine and Molière, whom he resembles in form as well as in point of view, and even Shakespeare, when allowances are made for the most extreme differences in subject and form. These poets are not, like Dickens and Hardy, writers of melodrama—either humorous or pessimistic, nor secretaries of society like Balzac, nor prophets like Tolstoy: they are occupied simply with the presentation of conflicts of moral character, which they do not concern themselves about softening or averting. They do not indict society for these situations: they regard them as universal and inevitable. They do not even blame God for allowing them: they accept them as the conditions of life.

It is also possible to see many of James's stories as psychological thought-experiments. In his preface to the New York edition of The American he describes the development of the story in his mind as exactly such: the "situation" of an American, "some robust but insidiously beguiled and betrayed, some cruelly wronged, compatriot..." with the focus of the story being on the response of this wronged man. The Portrait of a Lady may be an experiment to see what happens when an idealistic young woman suddenly becomes very rich. In many of his tales, characters seem to exemplify alternative futures and possibilities, as most markedly in "The Jolly Corner", in which the protagonist and a ghost-doppelganger live alternative American and European lives; and in others, like The Ambassadors, an older James seems fondly to regard his own younger self facing a crucial moment.

Major novels

The first period of James's fiction, usually considered to have culminated in The Portrait of a Lady, concentrated on the contrast between Europe and America. The style of these novels is generally straightforward and, though personally characteristic, well within the norms of 19th-century fiction. Roderick Hudson (1875) is a Künstlerroman that traces the development of the title character, an extremely talented sculptor. Although the book shows some signs of immaturity—this was James's first serious attempt at a full-length novel—it has attracted favourable comment due to the vivid realisation of the three major characters: Roderick Hudson, superbly gifted but unstable and unreliable; Rowland Mallet, Roderick's limited but much more mature friend and patron; and Christina Light, one of James's most enchanting and maddening femmes fatales. The pair of Hudson and Mallet has been seen as representing the two sides of James's own nature: the wildly imaginative artist and the brooding conscientious mentor.

In The Portrait of a Lady (1881) James concluded the first phase of his career with a novel that remains his most popular piece of long fiction. The story is of a spirited young American woman, Isabel Archer, who "affronts her destiny" and finds it overwhelming. She inherits a large amount of money and subsequently becomes the victim of Machiavellian scheming by two American expatriates. The narrative is set mainly in Europe, especially in England and Italy. Generally regarded as the masterpiece of his early phase, The Portrait of a Lady is described as a psychological novel, exploring the minds of his characters, and almost a work of social science, exploring the differences between Europeans and Americans, the old and the new worlds.

The second period of James's career, which extends from the publication of The Portrait of a Lady through the end of the nineteenth century, features less popular novels including The Princess Casamassima, published serially in The Atlantic Monthly in 1885–1886, and The Bostonians, published serially in The Century Magazine during the same period. This period also featured James's celebrated Gothic novella, The Turn of the Screw.

The third period of James's career reached its most significant achievement in three novels published just around the start of the 20th century: The Wings of the Dove (1902), The Ambassadors (1903), and The Golden Bowl (1904). Critic F. O. Matthiessen called this "trilogy" James's major phase, and these novels have certainly received intense critical study. It was the second-written of the books, The Wings of the Dove (1902) that was the first published because it attracted no serialization. This novel tells the story of Milly Theale, an American heiress stricken with a serious disease, and her impact on the people around her. Some of these people befriend Milly with honourable motives, while others are more self-interested. James stated in his autobiographical books that Milly was based on Minny Temple, his beloved cousin who died at an early age of tuberculosis. He said that he attempted in the novel to wrap her memory in the "beauty and dignity of art".

Shorter narratives

James was particularly interested in what he called the "beautiful and blest nouvelle", or the longer form of short narrative. Still, he produced a number of very short stories in which he achieved notable compression of sometimes complex subjects. The following narratives are representative of James's achievement in the shorter forms of fiction.

- "A Tragedy of Error" (1864), short story

- "The Story of a Year" (1865), short story

- A Passionate Pilgrim (1871), novella

- Madame de Mauves (1874), novella

- Daisy Miller (1878), novella

- The Aspern Papers (1888), novella

- The Lesson of the Master (1888), novella

- The Pupil (1891), short story

- "The Figure in the Carpet" (1896), short story

- The Beast in the Jungle (1903), novella

- An International Episode (1878)

- Picture and Text

- Four Meetings (1885)

- A London Life, and Other Tales (1889)

- The Spoils of Poynton (1896)

- Embarrassments (1896)
- The Two Magics: The Turn of the Screw, Covering End (1898)
- A Little Tour of France (1900)
- The Sacred Fount (1901)
- Views and Reviews (1908)
- The Wings of the Dove, Volume I (1902)
- The Wings of the Dove, Volume II (1909)
- The Finer Grain (1910)
- The Outcry (1911)
- Lady Barbarina: The Siege of London, An International Episod and Other Tales (1922)
- The Birthplace (1922)

Plays

At several points in his career James wrote plays, beginning with one-ac plays written for periodicals in 1869 and 1871 and a dramatisation of hi popular novella Daisy Miller in 1882. From 1890 to 1892, having receive a bequest that freed him from magazine publication, he made a strenuou effort to succeed on the London stage, writing a half-dozen plays of whic only one, a dramatisation of his novel The American, was produced. This pla was performed for several years by a touring repertory company and had respectable run in London, but did not earn very much money for James. Hi other plays written at this time were not produced.

In 1893, however, he responded to a request from actor-manage George Alexander for a serious play for the opening of his renovated S James's Theatre, and wrote a long drama, Guy Domville, which Alexande produced. There was a noisy uproar on the opening night, 5 January 1895 with hissing from the gallery when James took his bow after the final curtain and the author was upset. The play received moderately good reviews an had a modest run of four weeks before being taken off to make way for Oscar Wilde's The Importance of Being Earnest, which Alexander thought would have better prospects for the coming season.

After the stresses and disappointment of these efforts James insisted that he would write no more for the theatre, but within weeks had agreed to write a curtain-raiser for Ellen Terry. This became the one-act "Summersoft", which he later rewrote into a short story, "Covering End", and then expanded into a full-length play, The High Bid, which had a brief run in London in 1907, when James made another concerted effort to write for the stage. He wrote three new plays, two of which were in production when the death of Edward VII on 6 May 1910 plunged London into mourning and theatres closed. Discouraged by failing health and the stresses of theatrical work, James did not renew his efforts in the theatre, but recycled his plays as successful novels. The Outcry was a best-seller in the United States when it was published in 1911. During the years 1890–1893 when he was most engaged with the theatre, James wrote a good deal of theatrical criticism and assisted Elizabeth Robins and others in translating and producing Henrik Ibsen for the first time in London.

Leon Edel argued in his psychoanalytic biography that James was traumatised by the opening night uproar that greeted Guy Domville, and that it plunged him into a prolonged depression. The successful later novels, in Edel's view, were the result of a kind of self-analysis, expressed in fiction, which partly freed him from his fears. Other biographers and scholars have not accepted this account, however; the more common view being that of F.O. Matthiessen, who wrote: "Instead of being crushed by the collapse of his hopes [for the theatre]... he felt a resurgence of new energy."

Non-fiction

Beyond his fiction, James was one of the more important literary critics in the history of the novel. In his classic essay The Art of Fiction (1884), he argued against rigid prescriptions on the novelist's choice of subject and method of treatment. He maintained that the widest possible freedom in content and approach would help ensure narrative fiction's continued vitality.

89

James wrote many valuable critical articles on other novelists; typical is his book-length study of Nathaniel Hawthorne, which has been the subject of critical debate. Richard Brodhead has suggested that the study was emblematic of James's struggle with Hawthorne's influence, and constituted an effort to place the elder writer "at a disadvantage." Gordon Fraser, meanwhile, has suggested that the study was part of a more commercial effort by James to introduce himself to British readers as Hawthorne's natural successor.

When James assembled the New York Edition of his fiction in his final years, he wrote a series of prefaces that subjected his own work to searching, occasionally harsh criticism.

At 22 James wrote The Noble School of Fiction for The Nation's first issue in 1865. He would write, in all, over 200 essays and book, art, and theatre reviews for the magazine.

For most of his life James harboured ambitions for success as a playwright. He converted his novel The American into a play that enjoyed modest returns in the early 1890s. In all he wrote about a dozen plays, most of which went unproduced. His costume drama Guy Domville failed disastrously on its opening night in 1895. James then largely abandoned his efforts to conquer the stage and returned to his fiction. In his Notebooks he maintained that his theatrical experiment benefited his novels and tales by helping him dramatise his characters' thoughts and emotions. James produced a small but valuable amount of theatrical criticism, including perceptive appreciations of Henrik Ibsen.

With his wide-ranging artistic interests, James occasionally wrote on the visual arts. Perhaps his most valuable contribution was his favourable assessment of fellow expatriate John Singer Sargent, a painter whose critical status has improved markedly in recent decades. James also wrote sometimes charming, sometimes brooding articles about various places he visited and lived in. His most famous books of travel writing include Italian Hours (an example of the charming approach) and The American Scene (most definitely on the brooding side).

James was one of the great letter-writers of any era. More than ten thousand of his personal letters are extant, and over three thousand have been published in a large number of collections. A complete edition of James's letters began publication in 2006, edited by Pierre Walker and Greg Zacharias. As of 2014, eight volumes have been published, covering the period from 1855 to 1880. James's correspondents included celebrated contemporaries like Robert Louis Stevenson, Edith Wharton and Joseph Conrad, along with many others in his wide circle of friends and acquaintances. The letters range from the "mere twaddle of graciousness" to serious discussions of artistic, social and personal issues.

Very late in life James began a series of autobiographical works: A Small Boy and Others, Notes of a Son and Brother, and the unfinished The Middle Years. These books portray the development of a classic observer who was passionately interested in artistic creation but was somewhat reticent about participating fully in the life around him.

Reception

Criticism, biographies and fictional treatments

James's work has remained steadily popular with the limited audience of educated readers to whom he spoke during his lifetime, and has remained firmly in the canon, but, after his death, some American critics, such as Van Wyck Brooks, expressed hostility towards James for his long expatriation and eventual naturalisation as a British subject. Other critics such as E. M. Forster complained about what they saw as James's squeamishness in the treatment of sex and other possibly controversial material, or dismissed his late style as difficult and obscure, relying heavily on extremely long sentences and excessively latinate language. Similarly Oscar Wilde criticised him for writing "fiction as if it were a painful duty". Vernon Parrington, composing a canon of American literature, condemned James for having cut himself off from America. Jorge Luis Borges wrote about him, "Despite the scruples and delicate complexities of James, his work suffers from a major defect: the absence of life." And Virginia Woolf, writing to Lytton Strachey, asked, "Please tell me what you find in Henry James. ... we have his works here, and

I read, and I can't find anything but faintly tinged rose water, urbane and sleek, but vulgar and pale as Walter Lamb. Is there really any sense in it?" The novelist W. Somerset Maugham wrote, "He did not know the English as an Englishman instinctively knows them and so his English characters never to my mind quite ring true," and argued "The great novelists, even in seclusion, have lived life passionately. Henry James was content to observe it from a window." Maugham nevertheless wrote, "The fact remains that those last novels of his, notwithstanding their unreality, make all other novels, except the very best, unreadable." Colm Tóibín observed that James "never really wrote about the English very well. His English characters don't work for me."

Despite these criticisms, James is now valued for his psychological and moral realism, his masterful creation of character, his low-key but playful humour, and his assured command of the language. In his 1983 book, The Novels of Henry James, Edward Wagenknecht offers an assessment that echoes Theodora Bosanquet's:

> "To be completely great," Henry James wrote in an early review, "a work of art must lift up the heart," and his own novels do this to an outstanding degree ... More than sixty years after his death, the great novelist who sometimes professed to have no opinions stands foursquare in the great Christian humanistic and democratic tradition. The men and women who, at the height of World War II, raided the secondhand shops for his out-of-print books knew what they were about. For no writer ever raised a braver banner to which all who love freedom might adhere.

William Dean Howells saw James as a representative of a new realist school of literary art which broke with the English romantic tradition epitomised by the works of Charles Dickens and William Makepeace Thackeray. Howells wrote that realism found "its chief exemplar in Mr. James... A novelist he is not, after the old fashion, or after any fashion but his own." F.R. Leavis championed Henry James as a novelist of "established pre-eminence" in The Great Tradition (1948), asserting that The Portrait of a Lady and The Bostonians were "the two most brilliant novels in the language." James is now prized as a master of point of view who moved literary fiction forward by insisting in showing, not telling, his stories to the reader. (Source: Wikipedia)

NOTABLE WORKS

<u>NOVELS</u>

Watch and Ward (1871)

Roderick Hudson (1875)

The American (1877)

The Europeans (1878)

Confidence (1879)

Washington Square (1880)

The Portrait of a Lady (1881)

The Bostonians (1886)

The Princess Casamassima (1886)

The Reverberator (1888)

The Tragic Muse (1890)

The Other House (1896)

The Spoils of Poynton (1897)

What Maisie Knew (1897)

The Awkward Age (1899)

The Sacred Fount (1901)

The Wings of the Dove (1902)

The Ambassadors (1903)

The Golden Bowl (1904)

The Whole Family (collaborative novel with eleven other authors, 1908

The Outcry (1911)

The Ivory Tower (unfinished, published posthumously 1917)

The Sense of the Past (unfinished, published posthumously 1917)

SHORT STORIES AND NOVELLAS

A Tragedy of Error (1864)

The Story of a Year (1865)

A Landscape Painter (1866)

A Day of Days (1866)

My Friend Bingham (1867)

Poor Richard (1867)

The Story of a Masterpiece (1868)

A Most Extraordinary Case (1868)

A Problem (1868)

De Grey: A Romance (1868)

Osborne's Revenge (1868)

The Romance of Certain Old Clothes (1868)

A Light Man (1869)

Gabrielle de Bergerac (1869)

Travelling Companions (1870)

A Passionate Pilgrim (1871)

At Isella (1871)

Master Eustace (1871)

Guest's Confession (1872)

The Madonna of the Future (1873)

The Sweetheart of M. Briseux (1873)

The Last of the Valerii (1874)

Madame de Mauves (1874)

Adina (1874)

Professor Fargo (1874)

Eugene Pickering (1874)

Benvolio (1875)

Crawford's Consistency (1876)

The Ghostly Rental (1876)

Four Meetings (1877)

Rose-Agathe (1878, as Théodolinde)

Daisy Miller (1878)

Longstaff's Marriage (1878)

An International Episode (1878)

The Pension Beaurepas (1879)

A Diary of a Man of Fifty (1879)

A Bundle of Letters (1879)

The Point of View (1882)

The Siege of London (1883)

Impressions of a Cousin (1883)

Lady Barberina (1884)

Pandora (1884)

The Author of Beltraffio (1884)

Georgina's Reasons (1884)

A New England Winter (1884)

The Path of Duty (1884)

Mrs. Temperly (1887)

Louisa Pallant (1888)

The Aspern Papers (1888)

The Liar (1888)

The Modern Warning (1888, originally published as The Two Countries)

A London Life (1888)

The Patagonia (1888)

The Lesson of the Master (1888)

The Solution (1888)

The Pupil (1891)

Brooksmith (1891)

The Marriages (1891)

The Chaperon (1891)

Sir Edmund Orme (1891)

Nona Vincent (1892)

The Real Thing (1892)

The Private Life (1892)

Lord Beaupré (1892)

The Visits (1892)

Sir Dominick Ferrand (1892)

Greville Fane (1892)

Collaboration (1892)

Owen Wingrave (1892)

The Wheel of Time (1892)

The Middle Years (1893)

The Death of the Lion (1894)

The Coxon Fund (1894)

The Next Time (1895)

Glasses (1896)

The Altar of the Dead (1895)

The Figure in the Carpet (1896)

The Way It Came (1896, also published as The Friends of the Friends)

The Turn of the Screw (1898)

Covering End (1898)

In the Cage (1898)

John Delavoy (1898)

The Given Case (1898)

Europe (1899)

The Great Condition (1899)

The Real Right Thing (1899)

Paste (1899)

The Great Good Place (1900)

Maud-Evelyn (1900)

Miss Gunton of Poughkeepsie (1900)

The Tree of Knowledge (1900)

The Abasement of the Northmores (1900)

The Third Person (1900)

The Special Type (1900)

The Tone of Time (1900)

Broken Wings (1900)

The Two Faces (1900)

Mrs. Medwin (1901)

The Beldonald Holbein (1901)

The Story in It (1902)

Flickerbridge (1902)

The Birthplace (1903)

The Beast in the Jungle (1903)

The Papers (1903)

Fordham Castle (1904)

Julia Bride (1908)

The Jolly Corner (1908)

The Velvet Glove (1909)

Mora Montravers (1909)

Crapy Cornelia (1909)

The Bench of Desolation (1909)

A Round of Visits (1910)

OTHER

Transatlantic Sketches (1875)

French Poets and Novelists (1878)

Hawthorne (1879)

Portraits of Places (1883)

A Little Tour in France (1884)

Partial Portraits (1888)

Essays in London and Elsewhere (1893)

Picture and Text (1893)

Terminations (1893)

Theatricals (1894)

Theatricals: Second Series (1895)

Guy Domville (1895)

The Soft Side (1900)

William Wetmore Story and His Friends (1903)

The Better Sort (1903)

English Hours (1905)

The Question of our Speech; The Lesson of Balzac. Two Lectures (1905)

The American Scene (1907)

Views and Reviews (1908)

Italian Hours (1909)

A Small Boy and Others (1913)

Notes on Novelists (1914)

Notes of a Son and Brother (1914)

Within the Rim (1918)

Travelling Companions (1919)

Notebooks (various, published posthumously)

The Middle Years (unfinished, published posthumously 1917)

A Most Unholy Trade (1925, published posthumously)

The Art of the Novel : Critical Prefaces (1934)